SECOND CHANCE AT FIRST LOVE

MARION KUMMEROW

Second Chance at First Love

Marion Kummerow

This is a work of fiction. All characters, names, and places in this book exist only within the author's imagination. Any resemblance to actual persons or locations is purely coincidental.

Cover Design by http://www.StunningBookCovers.com

MARION'S READER GROUP

Sign up to my reader group and download my short story DOWNED OVER GERMANY for free.

It tells you the story of Tom Westlake, British RAF Pilot story, before he met one of the Klausen sisters in my War Girl Historical Fiction Series and fell in love with her.

http://kummerow.info/newsletter-2

CHAPTER 1

July 1945 near the town of Lodz in Poland

Stan Zdanek stared at the burnt remains of his parents' farmhouse, swallowing hard. The lump of entwined emotions wouldn't go down as memories assailed him. Those happy childhood days he'd spent with his twin brother Jarek and his younger sister Katrina, the three of them always up to mischief.

Jarek is dead, he thought bitterly. And he hadn't seen his sister since that fateful day when they'd all had to flee after helping their Jewish sister-in-law Agnieska escape from the Ghetto in Lodz. Had any one of them survived the brutal war? Would they return to the family farm one day? Would life ever be good again? Would *he* ever be happy again?

He looked down at his wooden leg and cursed his fate. Cursed the war. Cursed the Nazis. After a shudder of self-pity mixed with rage, Stan shook his fist into the sky, angry with God Himself. A deep sigh escaped his throat as his gaze wandered to the fields behind the house. They extended all the way up to the nearby forest. At this time of year they should be in full bloom, bearing the heavy load of crops to feed hungry mouths during the upcoming winter. But the fields lay barren, weeds covering the space usually filled with wheat, corn, and potatoes.

With some difficulty he rounded the small farmhouse, climbing across fallen bricks and beams. Shielding his eyes from the scorching sun, he looked up. Parts of the roof were missing, along with the front wall. He narrowed his eyes at the charred pile of rubble on the ground.

Hot shudders of rage ran down his spine as he remembered how the Nazis had torched the house. The smell of burnt ashes seemed to still linger in the air, even after more than a year had passed. A year that seemed like an entire lifetime. He scoffed, the suppressed rage bubbling up, boiling his blood.

If only–

If only things had been different.

If only he hadn't been shot, captured and lost his damn leg.

He'd returned home hoping – what? To find peace? Officially, peace prevailed since Germany's unconditional surrender on May 8th, but Stan's soul was caught in inner turmoil. He'd hoped returning to the farm would somehow ease the pain. But now, gaping at the charred disaster the Nazis had left behind, he seriously doubted his own sanity. He bumped his fist into the wall with a hapless scream, causing mortar to trickle down. There wasn't much left of the house, certainly no reminder of happier days.

Stan entered the house through the gaping hole in the

front wall as if the door were still hanging on its hinges. Rubble, dust, dirt, and dead leaves covered the floor along with the evidence of rodents who'd made the house theirs.

Another groan escaped his throat, but this time he knew better than to punch the damaged wall. It would take weeks of hard work before he could even consider it a *house*. The massive wooden kitchen table had burnt to ashes along with the rest of the furniture downstairs. Only the brick and metal stove had survived more or less unscathed.

Hesitantly, and not because of his missing leg, he glanced at the stairs to the second floor. How much more destruction would he discover up there? With trepidation he climbed up, one slow and careful step on the stone stairs after another. Bright sunlight blinded him as he stepped onto the roofless upstairs level.

The walls appeared to be in good enough shape, but without the protection of a roof, the floor had been exposed to the elements. The remains of birds' nests littered the hardwood and the support beams for the roofing had been reduced to charcoaled trunks. They'd have to be replaced before he could even think of repairing the roof.

A wave of helplessness hit him and quickly turned into red-hot rage again. He couldn't do it. He couldn't even repair his own roof. He wasn't a real man anymore. Running a hand across the full blond beard covering his face, he turned around and carefully made his way downstairs.

Most of the windows in the first floor had been blown out, glass splinters still covering the ground. As far as he could see the only intact place in the entire house was the tiny space beneath the stone staircase, just big enough for a small person to lie down. Not him, though. He'd have to find another place to sleep.

Suddenly a feeling of depression overcame him and he fled through the charred remains of the back door into the backyard, where he stopped in utter shock. His late mother's vegetable and herb garden was in full bloom. Ripe red tomatoes hung in thick panicles, their sweet-herb scent wafting over, making his mouth water and reminding him that he hadn't eaten all day.

He walked inside the stonewalled patch and picked a tomato, savoring the warm and juicy fruit on his tongue. The vegetable garden flowed over with green beans, sweet peas, cabbage in every form and color, plants he recognized as carrots, potatoes and radishes. A smile appeared on his lips as he noticed the bright red currants on the ancient bush in the corner of the garden, only to be wiped off his face when he remembered Jarek and himself fighting over the last piece of streusel pie their mother had made.

He'd never fight with his twin again.

Wondering how all the plants looked so vibrant, he spotted the dented metal watering can, neatly stored next to the well, apparently in constant use. Someone must have been tending the garden. The need to pee didn't let him ponder the mystery for long and he walked to the outhouse at the far end of the garden. On the way back to the house, his gaze fell on the tool shed. A cursory glance revealed it hadn't caught fire.

He walked over and found the shed empty except for a few tools, but with the walls and roof intact. He decided to make it his home for now. He'd be perfectly fine inside the shed, protected from rain and wind... until winter arrived.

Stan shook his head in a gruff gesture. He'd worry about winter later.

With a sour grin on his face, he returned to the house, where he'd set down his rucksack with two sets of clothes, a thin sleeping bag, toothbrush, shaving kit and some provisions. Together with the dagger he always kept in its sheath tied around his hips and a few zloty notes, all his meager possessions were inside the bag.

Well, that and the family farm. Since his older brother Peter had decided to stay in Berlin and try his luck there… and Jarek was dead... it was only Katrina and him. But nobody had heard from Katrina and he feared she might not be alive.

He rounded the kitchen stove and his gaze fell on the well-hidden trap door his father had installed before the start of the war. He forced the jammed door open and stared down into the gaping black hole. The hidden pantry seemed to have survived without damage.

"Damn!" Stan knew there'd be a lantern, and food, in the pantry, but how should he climb down the ladder? Another loud growl coming from his stomach sped up his decision to clamber down, and he emptied his rucksack before putting it on his back. Using the strength of his arms, he let himself down into the hole, feeling with the good leg for support, and then he more or less slid down the ladder, using mostly his arms to keep himself from falling.

Once on stable ground he turned around and fingered in the semidarkness for the lantern he knew must be there. He found it in its usual location and seconds later the matches next to it, and lit the lantern.

When the flame lit up the room he thought for a

moment he'd gone to heaven. *Thank you, Katrina*! His sister had left the small pantry overflowing with canned food, sacks of flour, potatoes, preserving jars with fruits, berries, and vegetables. He also spotted a canister with motor oil for the lantern as well as a several large bottles of vodka.

He packed some food and one bottle of vodka into his rucksack, put the lantern back on the shelf at the entrance, extinguished it, and then heaved himself up the ladder, relying solely on the strength of his arms. Back on the kitchen floor he sat down, wiping the sweat from his forehead, scowling at the wooden leg that hung uselessly from his body.

With the help of the nurses at the Charité hospital in Berlin, he'd learned to walk, climb stairs and even run, albeit slowly, with his wooden leg, but normally easy tasks like climbing a ladder had become huge obstacles for him.

How many times had he wished to be six feet under rather than a living cripple? Only the persistence of his nephew Janusz, and Peter's second wife Anna, had prevented him from putting wood behind the arrow.

He settled his stash on the stove, grabbed the bottle of vodka and two cans of Spam and walked outside to sit on the porch, where he used his dagger to open the first can of Spam. He ate with the hunger of someone who hadn't been properly fed in years and wiped his mouth with the back of his hand. Before devouring the second can, he opened the vodka, tipped the bottle to his lips and took a long pull.

Leaning against the outside wall of the house and glancing up at the sky, Stan closed his eyes as the liquor burned its way to his gut. Despite its being late in the afternoon, the sun still hung high on the horizon, and it wouldn't settle until around ten p.m.

He emptied the second can of Spam, taking ever-increasing gulps of vodka, wishing he could drink enough to dull the aching throb in his stump, and his soul. Finally, the lightheadedness gave way to drunken stupor and his mood plummeted. The cold breath of utter loneliness and desolation took hold of him, slowly spreading across his body until it occupied every single cell.

Emotions that had been locked up deep inside for much too long burst out, cracking his armor of self-control. With a heaving sigh of whirling emotions, he stopped fighting. Tears spilled and gave way to wracking sobs, as he wept for all that he had lost. His leg. His future. His happiness.

He wept for all who had died. His parents. His twin. His best friend Bartosz. His brother Peter's Jewish wife, Ludmila. The kind midwife Magda. And so many more.

"Why?" he screamed, shaking the half-empty bottle clutched in his fist.

He slumped down and tossed back another swallow of vodka, seeing his future in the bleakest of colors. He'd have to spend his days in solitude. No woman would choose a cripple like him. He was still so young, barely twenty-seven, and he'd never feel the joy of lying with a woman again. The thought had him breaking out into another wave of sobs, until the drunken stupor eventually tossed him into a tortured sleep right there on the porch, his chin dropped to his chest, his back slumped against the wall.

~

"Stan!" a voice called again.

Stan opened his eyes to tiny slits, but closed them in the same instant, when blinding sunlight hit the pupils and sent shockwaves of debilitating pain into his head.

"Stan? Are you alright?" the voice insisted and tiny hands grabbed his shoulder.

He tried to shake them off, hoping whoever it was would leave him in peace and stop shouting. The shrill voice sent needle pricks into every nerve ending in Stan's head. He fought the urge to vomit.

But the other person wouldn't relent. When the noise persisted, Stan finally cursed and cracked his eyes open. Slowly the small person standing a foot away came into focus. It took Stan much too long to recognize the neighbor's boy, Tadzio, staring down at him with a sorrowful expression.

"Tadzio, is that you?" Stan asked.

"Yes. You're back! You survived!" The boy made to hug Stan, but he held up a hand, keeping him at a safe distance.

"Slow down. I'm a bit ruffled." Stan scrubbed a dirty hand over his beard and grimaced at the pain following the movement.

Tadzio's gaze fell on the empty bottle and he stared at Stan. "You drank all of this?"

"I guess it was a bit too much," Stan said, trying a small grin. But even this tiny movement caused another wave of needle pricks to his head. "What are you doing over here?"

Tadzio grinned and then pointed to the vegetable garden. "I came to water the plants and remove the weeds."

"The garden is your doing?" Stan asked, looking at the boy carefully and wondering how old he was now. Ten.

Eleven. Deciding he was no judge of a child's age, he asked, "How old are you?"

"Thirteen. I'm almost a man." Tadzio proudly puffed out his chest.

Not quite. Stan didn't voice his opinion, however, respecting the pride in the boy's face.

"I'm sorry about the house. There wasn't much we could do with the Nazis around. At least the fire didn't spread to the garden and the shed. When the soldiers finally left, my mom and I doused the embers." The boy shrugged, giving an apologetic glance. "We ate the produce and used your garden…"

Stan looked from the thriving garden to the barren plot of land behind the stonewall and said, "It's alright. The food wouldn't have served anyone rotting on the ground, now would it?" *Although I sure would have liked a bite or two last winter when I was in that hellish Nazi prisoner camp.*

"Right, yes? That's what my mom said. And we always hoped you and Katrina would return. So we kept the garden tended."

Stan's face darkened into a scowl at the mention of his sister. He still had no idea whether she was dead or alive. The uncertainty pained him, plucking at what was left of his heart. Not knowing was even worse than knowing… He peered past Tadzio and the thriving garden to the fields beyond. Fields riddled with weeds. It would require a Herculean effort to ready the ground for seeding. And it was already too late in the year for crops or potatoes. That ship had sailed months ago. If he'd come here immediately after the capitulation in May… maybe then he'd have had a chance at a decent harvest in the fall.

"We'll need food in the winter," Stan murmured mostly to himself.

"I will help you."

Stan stared at the young boy for a moment. "You?"

"Why? I'm thirteen. If you show me, you'll see how much of a help I am."

"Good, let's get started." Stan nodded and struggled to get to his feet. "Can you get me some water?"

Tadzio grinned and left, returning within moments with a bucket of clean, fresh water from the well.

"The well's still working?" Stan asked with surprise, cupping some water in his hands and drinking deeply before using another handful to splash and scrub his face.

"Wasn't easy to fix, but my mom asked Old Jakub to help us."

Stan faintly remembered the man who lived about a mile further down the road. He'd been ancient even when Stan was a child, and he briefly wondered how the old man had managed to stay alive throughout the war.

"That is fortunate," Stan said, dumping the remaining water over his head and shaking it vigorously. Some of the water splashed Tadzio and the boy jumped back with a laugh.

"Would you like something to eat? I have brought some bread," Tadzio offered, pulling a cloth from his pocket and revealing a large crust of dark bread.

Stan's mouth watered at the sight and he eagerly nodded. Tadzio broke a piece of the bread off and handed it to him. After eating every last morsel, Stan dusted his hands on his thighs. "Shall we get to work?"

CHAPTER 2

Agnieska waited in line at the Red Cross office in Warsaw, wringing her hands for several moments before she clasped them together tightly and took a deep calming breath. Like everyone else queuing up, she carried a list with names of friends and family. Hoping, praying, yearning that some of them were still alive.

Bombs had killed her parents during Hitler's invasion in 1939. And she'd held her dying sister, Ludmila, in her arms in the Jewish Ghetto in Lodz, but maybe some of her uncles, aunts, or cousins were still alive. Or at least someone from Peter's family, Ludmila's gentile husband.

A soft cry at the front of the line betrayed a young couple, the man's arms around the woman's shoulders as she surreptitiously wiped a tear from her eye. Another poor soul who'd exchanged hope for the dark certainty that the ones she loved had perished.

Agnieska wasn't sure what was worse, the uncertainty or knowing for sure that death had darkened her door... When her turn came, she swallowed back the icy fingers of panic that clogged her brain and her throat, and provided the staff member the names, birth dates and last known location – in most cases some concentration camp – of her relatives. One by one. Each time the woman behind the counter searched her many lists until she stopped the finger on the name, looked up to Agnieska with a sad expression in her face and said, "Perished."

The entire Soban family had been extinguished. Agnieska used all her determination staying in place, instead of turning on her heels and running away. But where would she go? After being given the name of Agnieska's last Jewish relative, the woman shook her head again and said, "I'm sorry. But there aren't many Jews who have survived. Is there anyone else you're looking for?"

"Yes. My sister's married family. They were gentiles."

The woman searched and searched, first for Ludmila's husband, Peter Zdanek, and their son, Janusz, then for his sister Katrina, but shook her head. "I'm sorry, but there's nothing here. You might have to come back in a month or two. We're still getting new information every day."

"What about Stanislaw Zdanek? He was with the Polish partisans…"

The woman searched again, until her finger stopped on the list. Agnieska held her breath. *Please. Please. Please.*

"I'm sorry…" the woman said and Agnieska almost crumpled into herself; "…that's so strange. Here's a Stanislaw Zdanek. He was a prisoner of war in a field hospital in Berlin. But then he disappeared. There's no trace of him since May this year."

Agnieska puffed out a breath, swallowing back the urge

to sob like the woman in the couple earlier. She stiffened her spine and gave the Red Cross woman a sad smile. "Thank you."

As she vacated her place for the next person in line, a sliver of hope entered her heart. Since none of them were confirmed dead, they might still be alive.

In that tortured moment, she decided that uncertainty definitely was better than knowing for sure…

She looked down at her feet, avoiding the eyes of the others in line. She didn't need to see their looks of sympathy or, worse yet, notice them avoiding her gaze so that they wouldn't have to deal with the pain she knew was written all over her face. After the atrocities of war, the agony of the inner turmoil disallowed empathy and taking on another's pain as your own.

Her head held high, she left the office, struggling to maintain her control. It wasn't that the news came as unexpected. She'd spent several years in the Ghetto and a forced labor camp herself. She knew the facts of life. It was a sheer miracle that *she* had survived.

The memories of Katrina's boyfriend, Richard – a German soldier no less – rescuing her from the Ghetto mere days before its liquidation came rushing back, hitting her with the force of a tidal wave. Her breathing became fast and shallow until black dots danced in front of her eyes and she quickly bent down to avoid fainting.

After a few long breaths she slowly straightened her back again and glanced into the sun high on the horizon on this hot summer day. I'm the only survivor of my family. *Why me?*

A shudder ran down her spine. *And now? What now?* She

had no idea what to do or where to go next, and during a short moment of weakness she almost wished to follow those who'd gone before. But then she balled her hands into fists, her fingernails digging deep into the soft skin of her palms.

She hadn't survived six years of immeasurable hardships, she hadn't defied the Nazis with every single breath, to leave this earth now without a fight. Life would go on. And she'd be a part of it. She couldn't change the past, but she had a future in front of her – unlike so many others.

Her feet automatically set into motion, returning her to the displaced persons camp where she'd sought shelter for the past weeks. It looked much like the Nazi camps where she'd spent all those years imprisoned, but less crowded, and with adequate food and health care. Yet it was still a camp, which meant it was nothing like home.

She longed for a home. Some place she didn't have to share with hundreds of strangers.

Looking at her meager belongings, she realized that nothing remained in Warsaw for her. Friends and family gone… her apartment bombed into ruins… no, there was nothing enticing her to stay.

A deep sigh escaped her throat, and then an idea entered her brain and lit up her mood like a ray of sunshine lit a room. She smiled. Yes, she'd go to the Zdanek farm in Lodz. She knew her in-laws had been forced to flee their farm over a year ago, but she hoped that if one of them had survived, they'd returned home.

Maybe she could find peace of mind in Lodz. In the company of family.

She packed her small bundle that consisted of a toothbrush and baking soda, a hairbrush, a piece of soap, two sets of undergarments and one faded dress.

Agnieska made her way to the central train station, buying tickets for the next train to Lodz. She found the platform teeming with people, including uniformed Soviet soldiers. A small shudder racked her body. By the looks of it, Poland had exchanged one occupying power for another one. *This is only temporary,* she thought. *When people have returned and all's settled down, the Soviets will leave and we'll be a free country again.*

One of the soldiers controlling the tickets smiled at her, and her first instinct was to duck her head, like she'd done all those years. But the war was over. She had nothing to fear anymore. She wouldn't let the past dictate her future. So she forced herself to smile back.

The soldier made a surprised but pleased face and came over. "Where are you going, lady?"

"Lodz," she answered, handing him her ticket. Her heart beat faster, despite her intention not to be afraid.

"Have a nice journey," he said, and waved her through the barrier.

Squeezed like a sardine on the wooden bench in the train she allowed her mind to drift to pleasant memories of her times at her in-laws' farm. Fourteen years ago when she was merely eleven, her family had spent a summer in Lodz with some friends. Her sister, Ludmila, six years older than her, had fallen madly in love with Peter Zdanek.

At the end of the summer, Ludmila had been pregnant. Nine months later Peter had moved to live with the Sobans in Warsaw, married Ludmila, and their son Janusz was born. Agnieska smiled. From then on she'd spent every summer with her sister and her in-laws in Lodz.

Hot days spent in the fields; afternoons in the big kitchen with mother Zdanek teaching the girls about herbal medicines, harvesting and preparing the garden's bounty; walking across the countryside after supper, talking about the future. And during one of those summers when she was sixteen, she'd taken an interest in Peter's younger brother, Jarek, two years older than her.

But war had chased away the pleasure of those days, and Jarek was killed a year ago. Still, Agnieska harbored a slim hope that somehow, she could find a way to recover even a small piece of the happiness from earlier days.

CHAPTER 3

Stan and Tadzio spent their days preparing the fields. Although Stan's parents had been healers, he'd learned the farmwork from his grandparents. If war hadn't interfered, he and Jarek would now own and tend the farm together.

Damn German bastards.

The thought of his twin still sent a stab to his heart every single time. Stan leaned on his spade and wiped the sweat from his forehead. Pronging the dry, rocky earth was back-breaking work. Add the scorching July sun and his missing leg to the mix and he almost despaired at the little progress he'd made. Glancing over at Tadzio, he saw that the young boy had yet again outworked him and pronged more than double the distance on his line.

Rage, mixed with helpless desperation, burnt its way through his veins as Stan stared at the wiry boy with the long, scrawny limbs relentlessly stabbing the spade into the earth. If he couldn't even keep pace with a thirteen-year old, it solidified his status as only half a man.

"Damn leg," he mumbled under his breath, taking up the spade again. With the good food Tadzio's mother cooked and the daily workout, his arm and shoulder muscles had almost recouped their pre-captivity strength. Despite being angry about his missing leg, he couldn't help but notice that at least his upper body was up to the task.

But as the hours went by, his stump started aching fiercely and Stan relapsed into an emotional tornado of grumpy self-pity. By now Tadzio knew better than to stick around when the angry beast in Stan awakened.

"I'd better get home to help my mom with the chickens," Tadzio said, shoved his spade into Stan's hands and rushed off before Stan could say a word. Stan glared at the boy's back, wishing he could make someone – anyone – pay for all he'd gone through during the past year.

He gritted his teeth and after working another half an hour he called it a day, intent on drinking himself into oblivion with the vodka he'd bought earlier this week. During the day he deluded himself into thinking he was whole, but as dusk settled over the fields, the certainty of being a useless cripple settled in like a dark cloud above his head.

Why am I even trying? There's nothing left for me on this earth. No happiness. If only... After eating the dinner Tadzio's mother had left on the porch for Stan – she'd given up on inviting him to her house after his numerous angry refusals – he usually fell down on the mattress in the shed, downing vodka until his eyes fell shut – often wondering if it was even worth waking up again.

Slowly walking up to the house with the two spades in his hands, he noticed a small person traipsing up the driveway from the street. He squinted into the waning sunlight and saw she was wearing a skirt. He watched her for a moment and then averted his eyes to concentrate on the uneven surface.

People like her happened along every couple of days. Displaced persons looking for a place to sleep or some food on their quest to reunite with family and friends. It seemed like half of Europe was on the move these days. Waves of refugees going from East to West, countered by those going from West to East. Floating leaves in a sea of destruction.

As he drew closer, he glanced up, surprised to see she'd rounded the house and let herself into the vegetable garden. She had her back to him, the faded grey-blue dress bagging on her skinny frame. Most everyone was skinny these days, especially the tormented people who'd miraculously survived the death camps, so he had no idea why her frail figure tugged at his heartstrings.

Observing her slow movements, something stirred in him and he felt a peculiar connection to her. He'd ask her if he could somehow help her along. Maybe she needed some food and water. Stan closed the distance in a hurry; strangely afraid the frail woman would vanish in front of his eyes.

When he was just a few feet away from her, his foot kicked a stone and the noise startled her, causing her to turn around sharply and face him. The spades fell from his hands and his jaw dropped to the floor. She was his sister-in-law.

"Agnieska? Is it really you?"

Her expression softened and she flung herself into his arms, pressing herself against him with such force he almost feared she'd crack his ribs. "Oh, Stan... you're here. I found... someone." Her voice cracked and he couldn't help but brush her long dark hair with his calloused hands.

"It's alright. You're safe with me," he said, holding her tight as a strange excitement built up in him. It wasn't merely joy about finding her alive; no, his entire body heated up, burning with desire. But as soon as he realized his feelings, guilt assailed him. He should be ashamed. No woman deserved to be with a cripple like him, especially not Agnieska.

But he couldn't drag himself away from her, as he should. Not when he relished her nearness, the warmth of her tiny body in his arms. The scent of soap on her hair. Another embarrassing thought caused him to cringe. He'd been out working in the fields all day in the scorching sun and probably smelled like a mountain lion. The thought of shedding his clothes and washing up didn't help to subdue his arousal. On the contrary, long-neglected parts of him sprung to life. Embarrassed at his lack of self-control, he quickly took a step away from her.

She gazed up at him from under her long black eyelashes and Stan watched a blush crawl up her neck and into her cheeks, before she looked down and straightened her dress. "I'm sorry for jumping at you like this... it's just... I thought..."

He knew exactly what she was going through. Hoping, praying, to find someone alive. The relief. The emotions bubbling over. A wide grin spread across his face and he cleared his throat, trying to put her at ease. Stan had never been good with people. That had been Jarek's job. But Jarek wasn't here. So he said the first thing that came into his mind. "You must be hungry."

"Always." She met his eyes shyly and the small smile on her face nearly undid him again.

"Me, too. There's soup. Let me heat it up for you." Stan ushered her into the kitchen and began to stoke the embers in the stove. Too afraid to give away his reaction to her presence, he turned away and said, "Make yourself comfortable on the porch. I'll serve you the soup."

She opened her mouth to protest, but shrugged her shoulders and left the kitchen. Suddenly he could breathe again. Back when they were still youths, he'd never seen anything in her but a friend. Even when his twin had a crazy crush on her, he couldn't understand what Jarek liked so much about the shy, quiet girl who never said or did anything to hurt another person.

Unlike him. He'd been the rebel not only of the family but the entire town. His volatile temper was well-known all round and had been the cause of many thrashings at school or in church. *Rebel. I was one of the admired partisans, fighting for my country against the Nazi bastards, and look what became of me. An embarrassment.*

Through the kitchen window he watched how she settled on the rickety chair on the porch. Just last week Old Jakub had helped him to organize a table and two chairs, but since the weather was so hot, he'd decided to leave them outside for the time being.

His gaze wandered around the big kitchen and he suddenly wished he'd taken greater care to try and clean up the house. So far he'd concentrated on salvaging the fields and had only done the bare minimum inside the house. When the soup came to a boil, he poured it into two bowls and carefully walked outside, balancing one bowl in each hand.

As soon as he reached the porch, her sweet scent attacked his nostrils and his heart raced faster than normal.

"Here's the soup," he said, putting the bowl down and leaving her again to fetch a jug of water and two glasses. On the way inside, he took a few seconds to will his desire for her to go away.

"Thank you," she said as he handed her a glass of water. Then she wolfed down her food with a speed he had never witnessed before.

"Hungry at all?" he asked on a grin.

Again, the cutest blush appeared on her checks as she said apologetically, "Bad habits. Eat your food before someone else does."

Stan wanted to stretch out his hand and touch her arm. Wanted to chase away the pain in her beautiful green eyes. Wanted to tell her everything would be all right again. But he inhaled to stop himself from blurting out his feelings and instead, he silently spooned the soup into his mouth.

When they'd both finished eating without exchanging a word, he leaned back and said, "I'm glad you're here."

An array of emotions flitted across her gaunt face. He knew about the Ghetto and her escape, but he didn't know what happened after he'd organized fake gentile papers for her and she'd left for Warsaw with his nephew Janusz. He feared she'd had to endure more ordeals, but while he wanted to know, at the same time, he feared bringing up dark memories for her if he asked.

"Me, too."

Silence ensued again, until he couldn't take it anymore and said, "I returned a month ago." She didn't ask, but her eyes the pale green of sea glass bore into him with so much tenderness he wanted to melt into them. Squinting his eyes for a moment, he decided to give her only the short account of his own ordeal, skipping the part where his leg had to be amputated. He didn't want her pity.

"The Nazis captured me when I was fighting with the Red Army and sent me to a POW camp in Germany. When the Russians liberated Berlin, I disappeared and lived with Peter's new wife and her family for a while." If she was surprised about Peter having married again after her sister Ludmila had died, she didn't show it.

"That explains it," she murmured.

"Explains what?"

"Why the Red Cross didn't have any information on your whereabouts."

"Why should they?" Stan rubbed his beard. He'd never even considered registering with them.

"I went to the Red Cross in Warsaw inquiring about my family," she said with a feeble voice, curling over on herself, wrapping her arms around her thin frame. It broke his heart to see the stark suffering on her face when she raised her eyes to him. "All dead. Every single one. Except me."

Stan could see the tears forming in her eyes and despite his intention to stay away from her, he reached over to hold her hand. An electric current passed between them and went straight to his groin. Agnieska must have sensed it, too, because she withdrew her hand and put it into her lap, her eyes big with confusion.

After a while she continued to talk. "Then I asked about your family, but they didn't have information on anyone. I decided to come here looking for survivors, because I thought as long as a person isn't confirmed dead, they might still be alive." A small smile lit up her porcelain face framed by chestnut hair. "I found you."

"You found me," Stan whispered, his eyes riveted to the expression on her face. He'd known her for more than a decade and this was the first time he realized that her soft red lips begged him to kiss them. He leaned away from her.

"What about... the others?" Agnieska's voice trembled with worry.

Stan grinned and said, "Peter and his new wife, Anna, are alive and well in Berlin. Janusz is with them. "

"Thank God."

"But I haven't heard from Katrina and Richard." A shadow fell over his mind. Not that he cared much about the man whom he called Fritz, but the thought of never seeing his baby sister again made him cringe.

CHAPTER 4

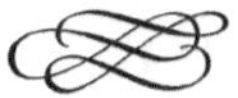

Agnieska stared into Stan's bright blue eyes, an unfamiliar heat seeping into her bones. She could feel the embarrassment flushing her face bright red. Here she was, having inappropriate feelings for the man who looked exactly like the boy she'd once fancied. Was this her warped way of honoring Jarek's memory? To throw herself at his twin the first chance she got?

The two of them might look identical, but their temperaments were polar opposites. Where Jarek was sweet, fun-loving and down-to-earth, Stan had a volatile temper that could change in a flash.

She glanced down at her hands, clasped together in her lap. And then up again into Stan's bright blue eyes. They'd used to sparkle with mischief, and occasionally they'd darken with fury. *Not occasionally, frequently,* she corrected herself. Back then every girl in Lodz, including herself, had been afraid of Stan's fits of rage. He'd never actually hit a girl, but his tirades of fury were legendary. As were his brawls with other boys, sometimes two or three at the same time. Usually Jarek, or their older brother, Peter, would step in and prevent the worst.

But now his eyes held a brooding darkness and pain. So much pain. Disillusionment. Anger. She yearned to ask what really had happened to him. But she understood his reluctance to talk about the horrific experiences he'd endured, the same way she usually blocked out the memories of her days in the camps. She had a future to live for and she wouldn't let the past ruin the rest of her life. Peace had arrived in Europe, and she intended to make the best of it.

"Thanks for not asking," she said, gazing into the familiar face, feeling a burning sensation in her stomach when he smiled at her.

"You don't need to tell me anything. We all have experienced things we'd rather not."

"That is true." There wasn't much else to say. To keep herself from overthinking the situation, she added, "Let me wash the dishes." And before he could protest, she jumped up with the plates in hand and rushed to the kitchen sink. She opened the faucet, but only a few drops fell into the basin.

"The water doesn't work," Stan commented as he entered the kitchen with a heavy bucket of water from the well. He stepped beside her and poured the water into the sink. He stood so near, she could smell his virile scent, combined with sweat from a hard day's work. It made her lightheaded and her body started to tingle in the most inappropriate places. She couldn't help but look at him while she whispered, "Thank you."

He doesn't look like Jarek. Not anymore. The Jarek she knew was a boy, but the Stan standing beside her was a man. A big man with broad shoulders and bulging biceps he'd undoubtedly gained by working hard in the fields day after day. The full blond beard and the dirt-smeared forehead only added to his rugged appearance, and she involuntarily licked her lips before she tore her eyes away from him and focused on the dishes in the sink. But the image of his face with the cropped blond hair and the enticing blue eyes had been burnt into her mind.

"I'll dry the dishes," he said and took a plate from her fingers with his huge hands. The accidental touch made her skin tingle again and for a moment she gave in to the urge to look at him. Her gaze travelled all the way up his bronze arm with the well-defined muscles, to his broad shoulders and down his torso, hidden by a greyish shirt. Even with the shirt on she could see he was still much too thin for his height of more than six feet, probably courtesy of the starvation diet in the prisoner camp.

Just looking at him made her want to be held in his arms, pressed against his broad chest. She shook her head, trying to rid herself of these most inappropriate thoughts. Suddenly she wanted to tell him. Wanted to get it off her chest. It was a frightening idea to tell another soul about her horrific experiences, but she felt she needed to do this to be free again. For some reason she didn't understand, she trusted Stan. Would trust him with all her pain and sorrow.

She scrubbed the soup pot like she wanted to make it shine and began talking: "Janusz and I were fine in Warsaw for a while with the fake Gentile papers you organized for us." She scrubbed harder. "During the Warsaw Uprising your brother Peter found us."

"I know," Stan said.

"After the uprising, we were put into a transit camp and one day they came for me and put me on a train to Dresden to a slave labor camp." Her voice almost broke as she remembered her frantic attempts to stay together with her nephew. "They wouldn't let me stay with Janusz, because he was just a child. Children cannot work hard enough. You can't imagine my anguish when I had to leave him behind." A slight sob escaped her, as the guilt attacked again. The guilt of not having been able to protect Jan.

"He survived, that's all that's important now." Stan turned slightly and his gaze bore hot holes into her skin. But it got worse when he put his palm on her shoulder and said, "You did everything you could."

Electric zings rushed through her body, making it difficult to think, even to keep standing upright. All she wanted was to lean in to him, to feel the comfort of his hard chest. She swallowed hard before she continued, "Dresden was horrible. I was there during the bombing. The devastation. The fire. I still don't have the slightest idea how I got out of the burning factory." She shuddered, unable to continue.

"I'm so sorry," Stan said, reaching for her hands. He untangled her fingers from the pot she was holding and clasped one of the hands, palm to palm, wrapping his long fingers around hers. Agnieska felt a surge of warmth rekindle in her stomach. She stared at him for a long moment, soaking up the feeling of safety and peace that his presence wrapped around her like a warm blanket on a winter's night. Somehow he had the ability to make all her sorrows go away.

When he finally released her hand and put the dishes on the windowsill, her eyes followed his every movement. He limped, which she hadn't noticed before. Her heart filled with empathy and she wondered whether the pain in his eyes had anything to do with the limp.

CHAPTER 5

Stan felt her eyes boring into his back and again he was embarrassed by the desolate state of the house. The kitchen still exhibited charred walls and a lack of cabinets, but he hadn't worried about those finer details. Over the last few weeks, he and Tadzio hadn't done much on the house but start removing the debris and assessing the overall damage. They had set aside the few salvageable things, but there was still no roof over the second story of the structure and therefore, no protection from the elements for those rooms.

At least they'd patched – with Old Jakub's help – the openings in the walls and had fixed the front door as well. But apart from those repairs he hadn't bothered with the house. All he worried about for now was getting the fields cleared and planted so that when winter came, as it was bound to do, they would have enough food to get them through until the weather warmed up once again.

He turned and his eyes locked with her beautiful

seagreen ones. The corners of his mouth tugged upward, but he pressed his lips into a thin line. Still, the urge to spend time with her was so overwhelming he didn't have a chance in hell to fight it.

"Do you have a place to stay?" he asked. Despite being sure the answer would be no, he held his breath.

"Not yet," Agnieska said, her eyes taking on a darker tone, as she continued in a lower voice, "I'll probably go into town and..."

"No!" He shouted the word, afraid to loose her comforting company. But seeing how she straightened her spine, he continued in a much softer tone. "Please. You don't have to go. You can stay here on the farm."

"I don't know..." she said, her voice small and shaky.

"Please. Stay. There's more than enough room." He made a grand gesture around the open-plan kitchen. But seeing the room through new eyes, he had to admit, it wasn't a very welcoming place. "Unless you mind the desolate conditions..."

"I don't mind," she hurriedly said, her eyes glued to his, making his loins pulsate. "But I couldn't do that."

"Why not?" Stan asked, feverishly trying to think of a way to convince her to stay with him.

"Because... because... I don't want to impose. I don't want to be a burden for you."

"You won't be a burden." *On the contrary, it'll be a joy to have you around.* When she didn't answer he added, "Where else would you stay?"

"In some displaced persons camp, I guess..."

Her tiny frame looked so sad when she mentioned the camp that she tugged at his heartstrings in a way no woman had ever before. "There's no way I'm allowing you to stay in a DP camp when you could stay here with..." *me,* he wanted to say, "...family."

"I... are you sure?" she asked, hope flaring in her eyes.

"I'm very sure. Please stay on the farm."

Agnieska paused for a moment and then nodded. "If you're sure you don't mind."

"I don't mind. I'd love to offer you a place to stay." *And have you around. See your sweet smile.* He watched her, the thoughts going through her head mirrored on her face and in her expressive eyes. It was clear she hated to seek out a camp. "Agnieska, stay here with me. Please."

She looked up at him and then slowly nodded, and the sweetest smile crossed her face. "Then, I accept. I have to admit the thought of going to another displaced persons camp is disheartening. They resemble the Ghetto so much and..."

Stan smiled at her. "That is all in the past now. You'll never have to go back to such a place."

"But my staying here is only temporary. Until I find a place of my own."

Stan's smile faded a bit. The thought of her leaving made him cringe. How could he miss a person who'd only just arrived? His train of thought surprised him; he'd never particularly wanted to be with company before. Except... Jarek's, of course. From the day they were born until the day his twin had been murdered, they'd been always together.

Shaking his head, he said with a grin, "I'll give you the tour. But don't expect luxury."

"Oh? And here I was thinking you'd offer me a palace with silk bedding and golden faucets." Her teasing smile brightened the room more than even summer sunshine at noon could.

After a rough day in the field, his stump was killing him and he longed to take off the prosthesis and scratch the scarred skin. But that would have to wait. He'd not expose his flawed body in front of her. Ever. The thought splashed iced water on his mood. How on earth could he ever have allowed fancying thoughts about desiring her? Even if, by some miracle, she might be open to his advances… no, it was ridiculous to think that he'd ever lie with a willing woman again. That boat had sailed without him.

"I've been spending most of my time getting the fields ready to plant. Haven't had much time to do anything in the house," he said with an apologetic tone when he led her around.

She stopped for a moment, cast him another of her loin-pulsating smiles, cocked her head and said, "I love what you've done with the place. This is an elegant blend of post-war and apocalyptic modernism, no?"

Stan froze for a moment as her words sunk in before he broke out into full belly laughter. The tension of the past years broke free, making him laugh harder and harder. After a few moments of bewilderment she joined him and together they laughed off all the hardships they'd experienced throughout the war.

Breathless and panting, Stan held his stomach and glanced at Agnieska, not believing his own silly behavior. How could a mere hour in her presence give him the peace of mind he'd been seeking for so long?

"I'm so glad you're here," he said, watching her blush at his words. Her deep pink cheeks had an unexpected effect on him as he wondered if she'd look the same when she was flush with passion. The desire for her surged with a power that almost knocked him down – and made him want to press her against him, showering kisses on her face and neck.

Stunned at the powerful emotions, a shiver ran up his spine. Obviously he had experiences with women, but he'd never felt such a tremendous connection to one before. He took a few deep breaths to regain his self-control and shove the inappropriate thoughts away.

She was family, for God's sake. *Related only by marriage,* a stubborn voice in his head said. *She needs my protection, not my assaulting her – Have you seen the way she looks at you? She's smitten – She's not. And even if she were, she'll be appalled as soon as she learns about my leg – You're plain stupid. – I'm not. It's called being realistic.*

Agnieska's voice interrupted his soliloquy with himself.

"I'm sorry, I didn't hear you," Stan said.

"Where do you sleep?" she asked.

"Me? Oh, yes..." He scratched his beard, having difficulties remembering what he needed to say. *Why can't she stop looking at me with her big green eyes?* "Sleep? Oh... I sleep in the shed outside. Haven't had the time to fix the upstairs bedrooms yet."

"The shed?" Doubt crept into her face and he could just *see* what she was thinking. That he expected her to share the tiny shed with him. Although he'd love nothing more, he quickly shook his head.

"Don't worry. I don't expect you to share a room with me." Laughter bubbled up from his gut as he watched relief transform her expression. During the tour through the house he'd been thinking where best to accommodate her. "Look. It's not anything fancy, but it'll be your private space." He led her to the staircase and pointed at the space beneath, not much bigger than a large closet, but big enough for a tiny person like her to stretch out.

With bated breath he waited for her to refuse and tell him she'd prefer the DP camp after all, but she nodded. "That will do."

"I'm sorry, it's not a real room, but—"

"Believe me, I've slept in much worse places," she interrupted him. "This is perfect."

"As soon as I find someone to repair the roof, I'll fix one of the upper rooms for you," he said.

"Why don't you repair the roof yourself?" she asked with an expectant look in her eyes.

Stan quickly averted his gaze, shame about his limitation creeping up inside him. Minutes passed without either one of them saying a word. He didn't want her to know. Didn't want her to pity him, to look at him the way people usually did when they found out about his missing limb. It was one of two looks: Disdain or Pity.

From her, he wanted neither one.

Her small hand pressed on his arm, and he glanced up to look at her thin porcelain fingers. So soft. So tender. So…

"You don't have to tell me, if it's too painful," she said, her sweet voice giving him all the reassurance he needed.

Stanislaw Zdanek might be many things. A coward wasn't one of them. He took a deep breath and decided she was going to find out sooner or later anyway; might as well rip the bandage off now.

"I can't repair the roof because they amputated my leg."

He watched her face as emotions flew across it. Shock. Sympathy. Compassion. Curiosity. Admiration. But nothing akin to horror or pity.

She looked at him, her eyes scanning his entire body and when she looked back up into his eyes, all he saw was acceptance and a warmth that hadn't been there before. He'd been so sure any woman would be appalled by him that he just couldn't wrap his mind around what had just happened.

CHAPTER 6

Agnieska recoiled inwardly from the revelation she'd just heard, not because she thought Stan was appalling, but because the news had hit her unprepared. How could he manage so well on his own with a missing limb? She hadn't even noticed. Soon admiration won over empathy.

"I barely noticed your limp," she said.

She saw how he puffed out his big chest a bit more at her words and the crooked smile on his lips made her tingle again in all the inappropriate places. This should not be happening. It could not be happening. She wasn't some floozy who threw herself at the first man who came along. In fact she'd never been with a man.

Her only experiences so far had been the hushed kisses she'd exchanged with Jarek a decade ago. Before the war. In a different life. When she was young and carefree. When she still had parents who didn't approve of their sixteen-year-old daughter kissing a boy.

She wasn't that girl anymore. But the sensations rushing across her body in his presence, made her dizzy, confused, and scared as hell.

"I'm sorry, but I'm more tired than I thought. Would you mind if I went to bed?"

"Off course not." His expression turned cold and he seemed relieved to get rid of her. "I'll leave a bowl with water to wash and a lantern in the kitchen."

"Thank you." Agnieska turned away to fetch the small bag with her belongings from the porch and returned to the kitchen, just when he entered with a thick blanket and a bed sheet in his hands, handing them to her. "I'm sorry, but that will have to do until I can organize a proper mattress for you."

"Stan," she said, looking at his tight jaw. "I really don't want to inconvenience you. And anything is better than what I had at the labor camp."

He swallowed hard, murmuring something that sounded like *I'm going to kill every last Nazi for what they did to you.*

"Sleep well," she wished him, faked a yawn and retreated to her space beneath the staircase. She wasn't really tired enough to sleep, but she needed time alone with her thoughts.

Finding Stan had completely confused her. Obviously she was overjoyed to see him; anyone in her position would be. She'd actually found a relative who had survived. But her current cache of turbulent emotions contained much more than happiness.

It was more like a warm, fuzzy feeling in her heart and butterflies dancing deep in her stomach. It was so unexpected because she'd always been afraid of Stan, even when she'd fancied his twin brother so many years ago.

Thinking about Jarek brought back old memories, and a few tears slid down her cheeks as she cried for what might have been. Hitler and his cronies had thoroughly messed up her personal life, along with the rest of Europe. With a sigh she sunk onto the blanket, covering herself with the thin sheet. It wasn't really necessary in the sweltering July heat, but she felt better covered from prying eyes in her small space beneath the staircase.

As darkness settled over the land, sleep finally claimed her and she drifted away, her dreams filled with future hopes instead of past nightmares.

The next morning, she rose when dawn broke and smiled when she heard Stan roaming about in the kitchen. She quickly pulled on her dress, combed her hair and opened the kitchen door a few minutes later.

"Good morning," he said, his jaw gaping open as he stared at her. She smoothed down her faded dress, wondering what was wrong with her appearance.

"Good morning," she said and stepped inside the room filled with the aroma of peppermint.

"I've made peppermint tea," he said, shrugging his shoulders. "There's no coffee."

"Thank you, I love peppermint tea." She took the mug from his hands, sipping the hot liquid. "Are those leaves from your garden?"

"Yes, just picked them on my way here." He'd also cut

bread, cheese and two tomatoes and put them on a plate. "Do you want to come to the porch and have breakfast with me?"

"I'd love to." She wanted to say so many things, wanted to thank him for his thoughtfulness, his hospitality, but for some reason, around him the words dried up in her throat. Her mind was filled with cotton balls and her tongue seemed glued to her gums.

They ate in silence and just when he got up to collect the dishes, she said, "Let me. Please."

"I can perfectly well do this myself!"

"That's not what I meant."

"No? You didn't mean to shower me with your pity because a cripple can't even carry his own dirty dishes?" The dark shadow of anger crept into his eyes and the pulsating vein on his temple indicated he was teetering on the verge of bursting into one of his infamous fits of rage. But Agnieska wasn't about to let him scare her, not anymore. She'd gone through far worse than facing Stanislaw Zdanek.

"Stop it, Stan. I do not pity you. On the contrary, I'm in awe. Look at you. You're toiling all day in the field to produce food for the coming winter. I would never have believed someone could do all this with an amputated leg." She smiled, suddenly finding the right words again. "Independently of what anyone might say, you are a hero. You must be the strongest, most valiant man I've ever met, even with a wooden leg."

"I'm not." His face had lit up with her praise, but he still showed a doubtful wrinkle on his forehead.

"What I wanted to suggest is my desire to make myself

useful while I'm here. So you can work in the fields, while I take care of the house. I'll clean, organize, wash, and cook."

Stan furrowed his brow, but after a few more minutes of brooding he finally relented. "All right, because you insist. But you don't have to."

"I want to," she said, keeping her mouth shut to the array of reasons she wanted to give him.

She watched him walk out the door, cross the garden, and take a few tools from the shed. Her heart squeezed tight with pity; not for his physical condition, but for the way it had hardened his soul and how he wallowed in a sense of inferiority. Why couldn't he see that even now he was more man than a thousand others combined?

A deep sigh escaped her throat, and she turned around, taking a good look at the mess in the kitchen. The entire place was in a shambles and wasn't actually fit for anyone to live in, but she still preferred it to seeking shelter in one of the displaced persons camps.

Deciding she didn't have time to waste, she rolled up her sleeves and got to work. She found a broom, brush and rags in one corner and walked to the well in the garden to fill the bucket with fresh water. Putting some of her precious soap into the water, she started to wipe down the grime from the walls, mopped the floor, dusted, and scrubbed until the kitchen shone with cleanliness.

Exhausted from the hard work, she stretched her back and arms before she instinctively ducked her head, fearing the inevitable whiplash coming down on her for taking a break. When nothing happened, she remembered the sweet bliss of freedom. The nightmare of being a Jewish slave for the Nazis had ended. Nobody would harm her.

Ever again.

Her growling stomach announced her hunger and Stan must be experiencing it even more so. She hadn't seen provisions anywhere in the empty kitchen, except for a few carrots and tomatoes on the windowsill. So she stepped onto the porch trying to figure out where Stan kept the food.

The sun blazed high in the sky, burning down mercilessly on the land beneath. She shielded her eyes from the bright sunshine and gazed at the fields, where she saw two people working side by side. A big one and a small one. Her heart gave a leap at Stan's familiar frame, but she couldn't make out the identity of the second person from this distance.

In the vegetable garden, she cut a lettuce head and racked her brain over how to make an actual meal with nothing but lettuce, tomatoes and carrots, when she remembered the hidden pantry beneath the kitchen floor.

Her neck hair stood on end as she opened the trap door and looked down into the gaping black hole. She really didn't want to go down there. Too fresh were the memories of her and Janusz hiding in there, hearing the hateful tirades of the neighbor Mrs. Kozlow. For a fleeting moment Agnieska wondered what had happened to the vile woman, who'd been an eager Nazi collaborator. These people weren't treated kindly nowadays.

She shook her head, reminding herself that the days of hiding were long gone. But as much as her rational mind tried to appease her, she physically couldn't set a foot on the ladder down into the pantry filled with ghosts from the past.

I'll just wait and ask Stan. Even while the thought calmed her own fear, she had to laugh at herself. She'd make him return from the field and conquer the ladder with only one leg, just because she was afraid of some unpleasant memories? If he could overcome his limitations, so could she.

Squaring her shoulders and taking a deep breath, she lit the lantern and stepped down into the threatening cave. With the flickering flame in her hand, the pantry wasn't half as scary as she remembered it from being locked up inside in total darkness, allowed to make nary a sound.

She grabbed several potatoes and poured two hands of flour into the bowl she'd taken with her. Today they'd have to be content with a potato soup, but she planned to make fresh loaves of bread the next day.

After finishing dinner, she walked outside to the well to wash up, careful not to be seen by anyone. Just as she finished, Stan and a thin boy with dark hair walked toward her from the fields. She waved at them, her heart giving another inexplicable leap at the sight of Stan's sun-bleached blond hair and the tan skin on his muscled arms.

"Hello, Agnieska, do you know Tadzio?"

"Nice to see you, Tadzio." She nodded, vaguely remembering the skinny, small neighbor's boy. But he'd grown considerably since she'd last seen him and also put on some healthy muscle.

"So you must be Agnieska, right? My mother will be so glad to hear you returned."

"Give her my regards and say that I'll go and visit her tomorrow," Agnieska said. Maybe Tadzio's mother, whom she'd seen only a few times before, could help her with getting this household stacked with the necessary ingredients to cook a decent meal. She turned to smile at Stan, who quickly averted his eyes when they met hers. "Dinner is ready."

"Dinner?"

"Yes, I made potato soup and—"

"You made potato soup?" Stan stared at her as if she were some kind of alien. "But… how?"

"I found everything I needed in the pantry beneath the kitchen."

"Oh." An embarrassed blush she couldn't quite understand flew across Stan's face.

"Will you eat with us, Tadzio?" she asked, not sure whether she wanted him to stay or not.

Being alone with Stan was so… comforting. Exhilarating. But also so confusing.

"No, ma'am, my mother will be waiting for me." Tadzio grinned and sprinted off.

Stan bent over the bowl of water on the well scrubbing his smeared face and hair clean. Agnieska stared at his back, and the pronounced muscles in his posterior, before gazing further down the dirty trousers and involuntarily comparing the right trouser leg with the thin, crumpled left one. Still, he was much more glorious than he gave himself credit for.

She held her breath while perusing his physique and when her eyes reached his shoulders again, he suddenly straightened and took off his shirt. The sight of his muscled back, crisscrossed by nasty scars, heated up the blood in her veins. The next moment he dumped the bowl of water over his head and her eyes followed the droplets running down his bare skin.

Thankfully, he stomped off to the shed, oblivious to her presence, and as soon as he was out of sight, Agnieska hurried to set the table on the porch. Several minutes later he returned with a clean white shirt with rolled-up sleeves.

"Thanks for making dinner," he said, sitting down at the table, wolfing down the soup. "That was excellent. Truly excellent." He observed her with a soft smile, one that made her insides go mushy, and all she could do was glance at her hands.

CHAPTER 7

"Look at me, Agnieska," Stan said, wondering why she was so nervous. Hadn't he just told her the dinner was excellent?

She slowly raised her head, and when her seagreen eyes connected with his, it hit him deep down in his chest. He wanted to take her beautiful face into his hands, kiss her luscious red lips... but that could never happen. It was entirely out of the question.

"Is anything wrong?" he asked her.

"No. It's just..." She clasped her hands together and confusion radiated off of her. But the moment passed and she squared her shoulders, raising her voice to say, "I have done an inventory."

"An inventory?" Stan leaned back in his chair, tired from the day of hard work.

"Yes, I went through the house, salvaging everything I could. But the yield was miserable. Two pots and a few pieces of silverware. None of the dishes were still intact. If we're going to stay here for the winter, we need quite a few things."

His heart jumped at the word *we*, but he kept his expression neutral. "What kind of things?"

"Well, mattresses, down blankets, winter clothing, cupboards, dishes, canning pots, basically everything." She produced a list from the pocket of her dress and read a seemingly endless list of provisions.

"Whoa. Slow down," Stan said. "I'm sure we need all of this, but one thing at a time."

"Yes, I'm worried how to pay for all of this and where to get the things we need, and I thought..." She looked so lost, it tugged at his heartstrings. He'd felt the same way when he'd returned to the farm several weeks ago, until he'd made the shed his home with the few things he needed. And food... he never cared about food, because he paid for Tadzio's help with produce from the garden and Tadzio's mother always made sure Stan wouldn't go hungry, either.

"Wait. I appreciate what you've been doing, but there's no reason to worry. Tomorrow you can ask Tadzio's mother to take you to the market in town. There you can sell our produce and hopefully buy whatever things you need to make this place a home again." *For us*. He longed to take her into his arms, to feel the softness of her body pressed against him again, but instead he shrugged.

When she gathered the dirty dishes he didn't protest. Ten hours of pronging the stone-hard earth had left him out of energy and all he wanted was to fall on his mattress and sleep. Minutes later she returned with a cold infusion made of lemon verbena.

"Here, drink this. You must be exhausted." Her smile

revived his spirits and he eagerly took the mug from her hand. The accidental touch with her soft fingers sent zings of longing across his body, making him stifle a groan.

"Thank you. It's nice to sit back and do nothing for a change," he said, looking at her. "I have no idea how Tadzio has any energy left to run home after working in the field for ten hours straight."

She broke out into laughter. "How old is he? Fourteen? You were the same at his age. Children have unlimited sources of energy, as long as they get enough to eat."

"He's fine," Stan said, instinctively knowing that she was talking about their nephew Janusz. Both of them had almost been starved to death in the Lodz Ghetto. When Richard had rescued them they'd been thinner than scarecrows.

"I'm sure he is, since he lives with his father now." Agnieska blinked a few times and then said, "I should go tend the garden."

"Let me help…" Stan made to stand up, but his swollen stump ached so much when he put weight on it that he groaned.

"Don't worry, Stan. It's not hard work, and you have done enough for today," she said.

For a moment Stan wanted to yell at her, demanding she stop treating him like a weakling, but he thought better of it and swallowed down his rage. The garden had always been his mother's duty. It should be Agnieska's now.

~

Stan paused for a moment and wiped the sweat from his forehead before it could drip into his eyes. Squinting into the blazing sun, he watched the dark clouds roll in from the east.

"Those clouds better bring us some rain, or all the work will be in vain," he said.

"Hmm… but first we have to seed." Tadzio didn't even look up from his work of planting cabbage seeds in the ground. Since due to the war they had missed the seeding season for crops, cabbage and other fast-growing vegetables were the only viable option.

"That's what we're doing, but we still need the rain," Stan grumbled, doing his best to keep up with him. He envied the stamina and healthy body of the boy. If only… Stan gritted his teeth. It didn't help to wish for his missing leg; it only made him depressive. Since Agnieska had arrived on the farm about a week ago, he'd felt lighter, happier. But many times a day he still wished for the mind-numbing effects of vodka to help bear his fate.

"Why don't we plant turnips?" Tadzio suddenly asked as he stretched his back and walked to the bucket to grab another handful of cabbage seeds.

"Because I hate them," Stan snapped at him. Seconds later he felt guilt over his outburst, but Tadzio seemed so accustomed to his mood swings that he didn't even blink at the harsh words. Stan tightened his jaw and growled at himself.

Several minutes later Tadzio returned for another handful of seeds and said, "You know, you don't have to eat them yourself."

"Eat what?"

"Turnips."

"Oh, you're still on the subject of turnips?" Stan asked,

controlling his voice as best he could. Despite his gratitude for Tadzio's help, that boy had the ability to annoy him with numerous suggestions until he'd burst out into a fit of rage.

"Yes." Tadzio stretched to his full height, puffing out his chest and setting his feet hip-width apart. "Nobody actually likes turnips, but people still eat them because they fill up your stomach and can be stored for months."

"Aha." Stan hid a grin at the threatening stance Tadzio had taken. It reminded him so much of himself at the same age. *Know-it-all. Unwilling to accept the wisdom of older men. Sure of his own invincibility.* He decided to indulge the boy. "So what do you suggest?"

"Well, to sell the turnips of course. Not in fall, not even in early winter – but in January and February when people have nothing else left to eat, the turnips will sell like hotcakes."

"Hmm." Stan knew Tadzio was right, but he hated to admit it. "Hmm. If you think that's such a fantastic plan, why don't you plant them in that row over there? I'll let you have all of them and do as you wish."

"You would do that?" Tadzio's eyes sparkled with joy.

"Hmm. Now go before I decide otherwise."

Tadzio leapt away and Stan bent over his hoe, waiting until the boy was out of earshot before he broke out into laughter. Tadzio could have his turnips if he wanted, but Stan wouldn't eat a single one of them.

Looking down the rows of completed work, he felt a sense of accomplishment. Finally. It had been a race against odds and time but now it was looking like luck – and the weather – was on their side.

In the distance a small person was walking up from the

house toward the field. Warmth flooded Stan's system and he automatically stood more upright. *Agnieska.* He still got ridiculously nervous every time she was around. Even now, as he observed the small figure becoming bigger as she approached him with his lunch.

Despite his protests she'd insisted on coming out and bringing him lunch every day. He grinned at the memory of their argument.

"I can perfectly well walk to the house and get my lunch myself," he'd said.

"Just because you can doesn't mean you have to, so please let me do this for you," she'd answered, meeting his gaze. Whenever she did this – the gazing thing – he became putty in her hands. How could he deny anything to the owner of those profound seagreen eyes?

In the end he'd succumbed to her wishes, grumbling, but secretly relieved that he didn't have to walk the long way up to the house and back. While he'd learned how to walk with his prosthetic on the uneven surface, his stump still got sore after a day's hard work. Not having to make the extra journey definitely had improved the pain. But he'd rather be shot than admit it to her. She had too smart a mouth, even without his indulging her.

Smart mouth. Beautiful, kissable mouth. Delicious mouth. Soft, red, enticing lips. He could actually *feel* how he pressed his lips over hers, capturing her moans of pleasure as he ravaged her mouth with his tongue.

"Hello, Stan," she said, interrupting his daydreams, and he quickly frowned at her in an attempt to hide the indecency of his thoughts.

"Thanks for coming out here. What did you bring?" he

asked, his stomach growling. He'd given her full rein over their produce and the money she earned selling it at the market. And he'd been surprised at how well she managed the funds. From buying necessary household items, farming tools, groceries, fabric for clothing to little luxuries like soap and toothpaste, she thought of everything and never once complained that there wasn't enough money for their needs.

"Stew with meat and potatoes."

"Hmm. It smells heavenly," he said, taking the thermos from her. "Would you sit with me, please?"

She hesitated for a moment, but then nodded and joined him on a fallen trunk at the edge of the forest. "Where's Tadzio?" she asked after a while.

"Gone to get turnip seeds."

"That's a wise decision. I wondered why you hadn't planted them earlier." Stan shot her a dark stare, which she completely ignored and continued, "You've made so much progress."

"But we need rain."

She squinted at the sun and then pointed over to the clouds in the east. "What about those? Won't they bring us rain?"

"I hope." He emptied the thermos with the stew and handed it back to her. "Thanks for the food. It was delicious."

A happy smile spread across her face and her lips begged him to kiss them. Stan blinked. Once. Twice. Her lips were still there. Full. Red. Ripe. "I'd better get back to work."

"Me, too. I'll visit with Tadzio's mother. She has offered to let me use her sewing machine."

Stan's gaze followed as she disappeared toward the house. It was hard to admit, but his life had considerably improved starting the day she'd appeared on his porch. The prospect of looking into her sweet face over breakfast provided his biggest reason for hauling himself out of bed each morning.

To smell the soap on her hair, the exhilarating rushes of longing he felt every time she brushed his hand… He might never be able to act on his attraction, but he could still try to be a better man – for her.

Observing her swinging gait, it struck him how content she always seemed, despite the awful sufferings she'd experienced. She'd never told him details, but from his own experience at the prisoner camp and the stories running around in town, he had a pretty good idea.

Nobody will ever hurt her again, he swore to himself.

CHAPTER 8

Agnieska walked back to the house in a happy mood. Bringing out lunch to Stan always brightened her spirits. She loved watching him as he worked, marveled at his muscular back and bronzed arms, his well-defined buttocks… a slight heat crept into her cheeks at those thoughts.

She shouldn't be yearning for the man who'd been kind enough to welcome her into his house. Especially not since he never showed any interest in her beyond being friendly. Not that she knew exactly how men showed their interest.

Entering the vegetable garden she picked a few ripe tomatoes with shiny red skin, lifted the tomatoes to her nose and inhaled the herb-fruity aroma. She closed her eyes and could almost taste the juicy, sweet fruit. Her mouth watered and she thought how she would have killed for a single tomato while in the labor camp… she took another deep breath, pushing thoughts of the past behind her.

In the house she dropped the produce into a bowl on

the windowsill and then gathered her sewing materials to visit with Malgorzata, Tadzio's mother. She took the shortcut across the fields instead of taking the road, not only because it saved time, but also because she secretly wished to see Stan again. The prospect of watching him move those impressive arms and shoulders was worth covering her shoes in stickers and soiling the hem of her skirt.

"Hello?" she called into the open doorway.

"Who's there?" Malgorzata's voice called back.

"It's Agnieska."

"Oh, Agnieska." Tadzio's mother came around the corner. "Come in. What brings you over here?"

"You kindly offered to lend your sewing machine, but if now isn't a good time..."

"Nonsense. Now's as good a time as any other. I'll show you." Malgorzata walked ahead, explaining the machine to her and then disappeared into the kitchen. Happily humming a tune, Agnieska used the foot pedal to move the needle, making a much-needed good dress for selling produce at the market in town and a sturdy apron for the garden and housework.

As always her thoughts circled around Stan. One moment he could be the sweetest fellow, and she even hoped he might find her attractive, but the next moment he reverted back to his grumpy and bitter self, making her feel like an unwelcome intruder.

Her logic told her that his mood swings had nothing to do with her, but more with his perception of being a useless cripple without his leg. But blame won the war of emotions, pointing its finger straight at her. She was getting tired of his behavior and of walking on eggshells around him, lest she evoke his wrath.

If only she knew how to help him with whatever struggles he was trying to deal with, but he wasn't talking to her. She gave a deep sigh. Everything had been so much easier before the war.

"What has you so worried?" Malgorzata said as she entered the room with two glasses of peppermint water.

"Oh… nothing. The usual worries about food and money." Agnieska wished she could talk to Tadzio's mother woman to woman. But although they'd become friends in the past weeks, they weren't close enough to divulge important personal matters.

"Food and money is always lacking. Without the produce Stanislaw gives my son we would all be starving."

"Tadzio is earning it; he works like a grown-up man. And Stan will be eternally thankful that you and Tadzio tended to the garden, otherwise there wouldn't be produce to give away or sell at the market. And then he couldn't buy new seeds…" Agnieska broke off. It would have been so much harder for everyone.

"We all believed everything would miraculously get better after the war, didn't we? And some things did, but there's still a long way to go until we have the same comfortable life we had before Hitler wrecked our country," Malgorzata said.

"You're right. And I shouldn't complain, since Stan so graciously welcomed me into his house."

"Stanislaw should be glad to have you. I was worried about him alone on that farm, with that… leg. Poor lad."

Agnieska nodded, although she didn't consider him a

poor lad. Seeing the pitiful look in Malgorzata's eyes she suddenly understood why he was so adamant about wanting to do everything himself. "He doesn't need me."

"Don't be silly. Everyone needs another person, especially men. You should have known my Andrej. He was helpless in household things without me." Tadzio's mother blinked a few times.

"Have you heard about him?"

Malgorzata shook her head and then said on a whisper, "What about your family?"

"All gone." Agnieska stopped her sewing and looked at the ceiling. "Every last one of them."

"I'm sorry. So many deaths. I'm glad the war is finally over."

"Me, too. But I'm worried about the communists, since they are Stalin's puppets," Agnieska said, taking the cloth from the sewing machine and turning it around.

"Shush… you wouldn't want them to hear you. There's frightening talk in town." Malgorzata looked over her shoulder as if she expected a communist to burst into her farmhouse any moment.

And how is this better than the Nazis? Agnieska bit down on her lips to keep the words captive inside her mouth. "That's why I prefer not to go into town, except for market days."

The older woman gave her a long glance before she said, "Unfortunately you're right to be careful. A woman in your position should get married to a good Catholic man."

"Married? Me? And whom should I marry?" Agnieska laughed out loud, but deep in her heart she knew that being married to a Catholic would give her protection from the still roaming anti-Semitism. She wasn't particularly religious and didn't go to church apart from the big celebrations like Yom Kippur and Passover, but that didn't matter to the haters.

"Stanislaw."

"Ouch!" Agnieska froze in shock and the needle pricked her finger.

Malgorzata smiled. "You shouldn't be so shocked. He always had a sweet spot for you. I remember one summer before the war, when he followed you everywhere like a puppy.

Agnieska focused on putting the needle back in place and moved the foot pedal again. For a moment she wanted to correct the other woman by explaining that she was confusing Stan with Jarek, but then she decided it probably didn't matter and she denied it flat-out. "Well, he certainly doesn't have a sweet spot for me now, because he's never said a single word to indicate interest."

"Sometimes a woman has to encourage a man to take the first step," Malgorzata said.

Agnieska felt herself flush bright red at the thought of such scandalous behavior. The memory of launching herself into his arms upon her arrival at the farm was still too fresh in her mind. What kind of harlot did such things?

She'd been so relieved to find a friendly soul alive, and since he looked exactly like Jarek, she'd forgotten herself for a moment. She hadn't been prepared for the physical impact the embrace had caused in her body. Since that moment, she constantly tingled in indecent places whenever she smelled his unique scent or accidentally touched his hand... or when she lay at night dreaming about his lips on hers.

The heated burning on her cheeks intensified, and she turned her face away from Malgorzata, focusing on her needlework.

"We're just good friends. He's made this very clear," Agnieska finally said. *Hasn't he shown time and again that he can barely tolerate my presence with his hot and cold behavior?*

"He may have said he isn't interested, but it's not the truth."

"Well, I'm not interested." Agnieska lied.

"You might want to change your opinion. A woman needs the protection of a man and you could do a lot worse than Stanislaw. He's a good man, even though he is damaged from the war."

Agnieska didn't answer and Malgorzata stood up saying, "Think about it." Then she left the room, leaving Agnieska alone with her thoughts.

Everyone is damaged from the war. Stan's damaged. I'm damaged. Even people like Malgorzata and Tadzio, who didn't fight, get captured, or spend time in one of the camps are damaged.

She had lived through horrible experiences in the Ghetto, had seen things she wanted to be able to unsee, had been forced to work from sunup to sundown with no hope of it ever ending, except through the escape death offered. Not enough food. No medical care, and sickness that swept through the encampments like fire.

Being treated as a subhuman.

She shook her head to ward off those unpleasant memories. The past was gone. She had to look at the future. A brighter future.

Some time later she finished sewing her dress and took

her leave of Tadzio's mother. "Thank you again for letting me use your sewing machine. May I do so again maybe next week?"

"Please. It's nice to have adult company." Suddenly Malgorzata seemed exhausted and depressed. Her husband was still missing and the only company she had was Tadzio and his little sister Lola.

Agnieska put an arm around her shoulders. "I will. It's hard on all of us."

CHAPTER 9

The entire day a nagging feeling of guilt plagued Stan. In his quest to disguise the attraction he felt for Agnieska he often overreacted by not putting his best foot forward. Whenever he did this, the hurt in her eyes almost slashed him. Telling himself her dislike of him was for the best didn't chase away the guilt. Groaning with despair he decided to do something nice for her.

When she returned in the evening from her visit with Malgorzata, he was waiting for her in the kitchen. The soup she'd prepared in the morning already simmered on the stove. She stopped in her tracks as she noticed the new cupboards and countertop.

"What's this?" she asked.

"What does it look like?" He couldn't help but flash her a bright and happy grin.

"Well. I know what it is, but where did it come from?" She still stood in the doorway, almost as if she were afraid to enter the room.

"I bought them from one of the merchants passing through on a regular basis," he answered. "You like them?"

"I love them!" He knew she'd been hard pressed to find a space to store things as well as a working area when she cooked for them.

"There's more." He was giddy like a youth, showing her what else he'd done.

"More?" Agnieska's green eyes lit up with joy, spreading warmth across his heart and stomach.

"Yes, come." He led her to the tiny space beneath the staircase that was now her bedroom – without a bed. "I got you a mattress as well, and a down blanket for the cold nights in winter."

"This is… wonderful. Thank you so much."

"You deserve it." He couldn't resist stepping nearer, basking in the happiness that radiated from her.

"Thank you. This is so sweet of you," she said, and he lost track of time and space. Somehow she ended up in his arms, her soft curves pressed against his body. His hands on her back, he sensed the little shivers running up and down her spine. The electric energy jumped over to him and his entire body hardened in response to her nearness.

Without further thought, he moved his hands up and down her back and she pressed even closer into him. Her sweet scent propelled his desire into unknown heights and he smothered little kisses onto her hair, feeling how her body softened for him.

His desire for her overwhelmed Stan. He buried his face in her hair, and simply soaked up her presence until he felt her hands wandering on his back, which encouraged him to continue the movement of his own hands down to her slim waist. If he wanted, he could span her waist with his two hands.

His heart melted with need and he couldn't help but groan. The sound seemed to send her off balance, because she took a step back and lowered her eyes as shame filled them.

"Don't run away, please," he said and tightened his arms, pulling her flush against him. She looked up at him with surprise that soon was overtaken by tenderness and... yearning. "Oh, sweet woman, I've wanted to do this ever since I first saw you step onto my porch," he murmured into her ear, caressing her back, her shoulders, and her waist.

She held onto him like he was her lifeline, and with every movement of his hands he sensed her heartbeat accelerating. Then he took her chin into one hand, and gazed into her eyes before he kissed her tentatively and tenderly. She parted her lips for him, but the very moment he ventured his tongue inside her warm and soft mouth, she frantically pushed away.

Her sweet face flushed with burning heat, he saw the confusion and embarrassment in her eyes and for a brief moment prepared for her fist to come crashing down against his cheek. Instead, she just took another step back.

"Agnieska, I'm sorry..." he began, only to watch as she ducked her head and rushed out the front door into the night.

Regret attacked him like a Wehrmacht soldier pouncing out of the darkness. He gave an exasperated growl and hit the back of his head against the wall, before he sank down to the floor. He was a beast. He'd basically attacked her, and if she hadn't stopped him, who knew how far he'd have gone? Agnieska wasn't one of the harlots hanging out with the partisans, she was a decent woman and deserved better than this.

Better than him.

He scrambled to stand and left the house through the back door, heading straight toward the pump for the well, filling the wood tub with icy water. As he climbed into the tub, the cold water numbed his limbs, but it didn't take the edge off his ravaging emotions. Even shivering in the cold with his teeth clenched to prevent them from clattering, he couldn't stop thinking about the heavenly feeling of holding her in his arms, her soft curves pressed up against him – the enticing little sounds coming from her mouth filling his heart and soul with desire.

Her luscious red lips appeared in his mind. How they begged to be kissed, and the hot and sweet desire raging through his veins the moment his mouth had connected with hers. And the expression of shock when she'd felt his tongue in her mouth. It was as if… no, that couldn't be. Had she never been kissed like that before? His heart rejoiced at the same time as shame spread into every last cell.

Even in the ice-cold water, he could feel the shame burning up his skin. What kind of man was he, treating her like a random floozy you could just kiss and have a good time with?

Much later, Stan was lying on his mattress in the shed, trying to figure out what to do. He would stay away from her – as far as he could. But the thought of her leaving the house made him cringe.

The house – I'm such a stupid idiot!

It was a miracle she was still living here, with the roof in a shambles. Weeks had passed and nothing had happened. Stan had lied to himself, that he was too busy to find and hire someone to do it for him, since he wasn't able to climb up there and fix it himself. But his excuses just hid the real reason, that he couldn't stomach the idea of hiring another man for the job. Apart from another lad's pitying looks, he didn't want Agnieska to realize the extent of his inadequacies. A real man should be able to fix his own roof. He shouldn't need help for such a simple task.

But that thinking was selfish. He wanted to give her everything she needed, and a roof over her head was one of the most basic needs of a person. Especially as autumn and winter approached.

Stan's brain ached from the complicated situation he'd maneuvered himself into. More than ever he wished his brother were still around. Jarek had always been the one to keep him grounded, to help cheer him up when he'd gotten caught up in morose thoughts. Without Jarek, he was just so… lost. And angry.

The thought of Jarek brought another stabbing doubt to his mind. What if Agnieska had shied away because she was still in love with his brother? What if she'd let him hold her just because for a moment she'd indulged in the illusion that he was Jarek? A cold wave of fear flooded him.

This woman had crawled under his skin like nobody else had before. She'd conjured up emotions and desires he'd thought long forgotten. At the age of twenty-seven, he'd resigned himself to living his life without his leg, and thus without love and physical intimacy. For a fleeting moment today he'd forgotten about his dark fate and somehow hoped the future might have something brighter for him in store.

CHAPTER 10

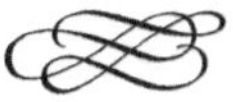

Stan's lips skimmed down her porcelain neck, nipping Agnieska's collarbone as they continued their downward path.

"I love you so much," she whispered.

He looked up and drowned in the depth of her green eyes. That woman had taken possession of his entire being. Heart, soul, and body.

"Nothing bad will ever happen to you again, not while I'm there to protect you." He rubbed his beard against her soft skin and wished he could remain in this moment for eternity.

She let out a high-pitched giggle, loud enough to startle him. Stan opened his eyes, his heart racing. He stared at the pitch-black wall of the shed, disappointed as he discovered it had been but a dream.

She deserved so much better than him. She was still young and had a life of possibilities ahead of her. Therefore, he had to protect them both from the emotions building between them.

In the dark hours before dawn, he made a silent promise. One she would never hear from his lips, but he meant to honor nonetheless. From here on out, he was going to care for her just like a brother would.

He wiped the sweat from his forehead and rolled over on his side, the house in his vision through the small window. He stared at it for a long time, unable to find sleep despite knowing that he needed to have his wits about him the next morning if he was going to exercise good self-control.

It was up to him to control the interactions between himself and Agnieska. The job of a man. He might not be able to repair the roof on his house, but he could control his baser instincts and protect her from himself. That he would do.

The next morning, the rooster at Tadzio's house woke him like clockwork with his cock-a-doodle-doo. Stan dressed, washed his face at the pump and walked over to the house, furrowing his brows at the morning dew on the plants in the vegetable garden. Fall would be here in no time at all and they needed the roof fixed by then.

The breath caught in his chest as he opened the back door and peeked into the kitchen. Agnieska was preparing breakfast and she was so beautiful in the morning light, Stan could only stand there and watch her. Snippets of his fantasy from the night before tried to sneak in, but he forced them aside.

She must have heard him because she turned around, her adorable face red with the heat of the stove where she was preparing fried eggs and potatoes. The expectation he saw in her eyes hit him deep inside, knocking the breath from his lungs and almost toppling his resolve to stay away from her. He hardened his heart and his features and said in a gruff voice, “Morning.”

“Did you sleep well?” she asked.

Stan ignored her question, settled at the table, and asked, “Is breakfast ready?”

“Almost,” she answered, giving him a quizzical look.

Stan nodded and all but tore the plate from her hands before she could even set it on the table. He ate quickly, his eyes fixed on the plate. Minutes later he finished the food she’d cooked for him without saying a single word, gulped down the cup of water and fled from her presence.

Even without looking at her face, he felt the tension oozing from her and he knew how much his cold behavior hurt her, but he held her best interests close to his heart. In his mind, there could be no future for the two of them and he refused to allow her to get hurt because of his rash actions.

CHAPTER 11

Agnieska stared with disbelief at Stan's back as he left the house, feeling completely out of sorts. Half the night she'd spent reliving the experience of being in Stan's arms and being kissed by him. Even now the memory brought a heated flush to her face. Oh... she'd never known a simple kiss could be as delightful, but.... she was a decent woman. She straightened her apron and busied herself washing the breakfast dishes. Decent women didn't let unmarried men paw them. No matter how much they enjoyed the experience. That's what her parents had taught her.

But your parents are dead. And times have changed. She gasped at the insubordinate voice in her head. The world would all be in an awful mess if people did not keep to traditional values and morals. Actually, the world *was* in an awful mess, because people had kept to traditional values like obedience and unquestioned authority of their leaders.

The second half of the night, she'd worried about how to

act around him in the morning and had decided to play it normal. Pretend the kiss had never happened. Revert to being friends. Friends, who looked out for each other, made each other laugh and shared the hardships of a farmer's life.

Unfortunately, Stan reverted back to playing his mood games. As he headed to the fields without even giving her a terse thank you for the breakfast, she clasped her hands together. What had she hoped for? Some indication that he loved her? She scoffed. Short-tempered Stan? An iceberg would melt before he ever admitted his feelings.

I don't know what possessed me to let him kiss me.

As much as she wanted to stay at the farm, she could not allow herself to become a burden to anyone. When the day drew to a close, she was no closer to having an answer than when she'd awakened.

Stan returned late from the fields, eating the dinner she'd left for him and then retiring to the shed. Agnieska remained in the makeshift bedroom he'd fixed for her, her heart heavy with pain. Avoiding him seemed to be the best course of action to take, at least until she got a clearer picture about her plans for the future.

Thus, they lived in the same place, but never exchanged a single word, or a glance, avoiding each other as much as humanly possible. She still made breakfast and dinner for him, but disappeared from the kitchen when she heard him step onto the porch.

Maybe it was her imagination, but he suddenly trampled with the force of an elephant, as if to warn her of his arrival. At noon, she still went out to the field, bringing him lunch, her heart weeping when she watched his strong body work the earth. But she always cast her eyes down as she neared him, set the lunch down in the shadow under the trees without waiting for him to approach. Which he never did. He pretended to be too busy to notice her, but she felt his piercing gaze boring holes into her back on her way back to the house.

~

Stan was having second thoughts about his plan to stay away from Agnieska. The tension between them was unbearable. The hurt and sadness in her eyes slashed his heart in more painful ways than even the worst Nazi treatment had ever done.

He couldn't stand seeing her like this. Hundreds of times, he'd almost reached out to wrap his arms around her and apologize. But that would defeat the purpose. She'd get over him soon and then she'd be free to lead a better life.

Without him.

With a man who could give her all she wanted. All she needed.

"Hey, Stan. We need to get that tree stump out of the ground." Tadzio's voice shook him from his thoughts.

Stan landed back in the present and looked at the stump in question. "I've got it. Why don't you finish up this row and then start cleaning out the ditch at the end? We could get this field planted before the week's out."

"Sounds good."

Stan grabbed the shovel and the axe and headed to where a large stump was sticking up from the ground. It was only about twelve inches across and he and Tadzio had already dug around the surface roots. The only task left was to cut those roots and then push it out of the ground.

He started hacking away at the surface roots, cutting through the three-inch-round roots until they gave way. Sweat ran in rivulets down his forehead and his back, but he was determined to win the fight against the trunk.

With clenched teeth, he ignored the pulsating ache in his leg and bent over, putting his shoulder against the stump and shoving with all of his might. He wasn't prepared to lose his footing and down he went, crashing down on the point where the prosthetic met his skin.

"Ouch!" Stan screamed with excruciating pain, loud enough to wake the dead.

Tadzio ran toward him, witnessing the debacle as Stan lay helpless, face down in the dirt, red-hot rage slowly displacing the pain. "Are you alright?" the boy asked with a worried tone.

"I'm fine," Stan growled and moved his head to see the young boy peering down at him. Another wave of agony hit him, until black stars danced in front of his eyes.

"Here, take my hand and I'll help you up."

"I can do it alone!" He hissed through clenched teeth although he knew perfectly well that he couldn't.

"Sure you can, but it's easier if I help you up," Tadzio said.

There wasn't much Stan could argue about, so he clasped the outstretched hand and let Tadzio pull him upright.

"Fu… uck!" He screamed again at the agonizing pain in his stump. "Sorry for that," he managed to say after seeing Tadzio's wide-eyed stare.

Tadzio nodded, cowed by the outburst, and Stan promised himself to watch his language – and his temper – better in the future. He didn't want the boy to be afraid of him.

"I'm sorry, I didn't mean to scream at you, but that hurt like… hell," Stan said, still reeling from the torturous ache.

"Want me to work on the tree stump?"

"That's probably the best." Stan cast his eyes downward, ashamed that he had to ask a thirteen-year-old boy to first help him up and then to finish the task Stan had been supposed to carry out. Without another word he turned on his heel and walked towards the house, limping more than usual.

About halfway to the house he remembered that he and Agnieska weren't talking. Swearing and growling he pondered what to do when she unexpectedly appeared behind the stone wall of the vegetable garden. He almost bumped into her.

"What happened?" Agnieska asked, nodding at his wooden leg.

"Nothing," he growled, glaring daggers at her. She disappeared inside the house and he flopped down at the table on the porch. Why did she always have to butt into his business? Why did she always want to make sure he was okay? *Women*! He was better off without her.

When she returned several minutes later and put a steaming hot bowl of stew in front of him, he automatically reached out and grabbed her hand, but quickly move his own hand away like he'd touched hot coals.

"Look, Agnieska, I'm sorry. It's just…" How on earth was

a man supposed to say that despite burning up with desire for a woman, he could never act on his attraction?

"Just what?" Her green eyes softened and she had him there again, making his lips tremble and his heart ache.

"I… I… You… Oh, shit!" He rubbed his bearded chin. "It's just… I like having your company." A smile brightened her face. "But…" The light dimmed. "…there can never be anything between us except friendship."

"Why?" she whispered.

"Because… because after all you've gone through, the abuse you've suffered at the hands of the Nazis, you deserve a bright future. You deserve a man who can protect you, provide for you, and give you everything you desire. You don't deserve to be bound to a cripple like me!"

"Stan, please—"

"Go. Please go and leave me alone."

She sneaked away, leaving him alone. Immediately, he mourned her loss, a wave of agony washing over him so hard he had to fight back the tears.

CHAPTER 12

The days passed, and the relationship between Agnieska and Stan returned to normal. Somewhat.

She still couldn't fathom why he believed himself worthless when all evidence proved the contrary, but he'd made his stance crystal clear. At least he didn't hold her responsible for her shameful tarty behavior the other day.

Despite his insistence that there could never be anything between them other than friendship, she found herself falling harder for him with each passing day. He made her laugh, outdid himself to make her feel at home, and even mentioned several times that he'd find someone to fix the roof for the coming winter.

One day in early September, yet another refugee in the never-ending stream of displaced persons that passed the farm knocked at the door. She was hanging up the laundry she'd washed earlier that morning and hurriedly rushed around the house to greet him. He was skeletal, with very short black hair and several missing teeth. And he had the prisoner-gait, the shuffling walk all the Jews had adopted in the camps to preserve the little energy they had.

"Miss, could you spare some water?" he asked with a voice hoarse from thirst.

"Come with me," she said, strangely affected by his big, sad eyes. Refugees like him passed through every day and yet, this man tugged at her heartstrings. She led him to the table on the porch and offered him minted water from the jar. He swallowed it in one gulp and sheepishly asked for another glass.

"Drink as much as you want. Water is about the only thing we have in abundance," she said, pointing at the well with the pump.

"Thank you, Miss..."

"It's Agnieska."

"My name is Amos."

"A Jewish name," she said, her heart filling with joy that someone other than herself had survived the Holocaust.

"That's because I'm a Jew." He bent his head as if afraid of her answer.

Fear not, my valiant steed! The words of an old poem came to mind and she smiled. "Don't be afraid. You're safe here. I'm a Jew myself."

"You are?" He looked up, his dark eyes filling with sadness, relief and yearning. "Give thanks to HaShem. There are so few of us who survived."

She didn't want to dwell in commiseration and asked, "Can I offer you something to eat?"

His eyes answered even before he opened his mouth and she said, "Don't deny it. I know hunger when I see it. Wait here." She hurried into the kitchen to heat a bowl of stew and brought it to him.

After eating his fill he looked at her and said, "How can I ever repay your kindness, good woman?"

She shook her head. "There's no need."

"Please let me show my appreciation. May I offer work? I'm a skilled handyman, and a woman on her own—"

"I'm not alone," she protested, "I live here with my brother-in-law."

"Well, then I'd better continue my journey."

"Wait..." Agnieska took pity on him and asked, "Do you know how to repair a roof? Or, in this case, build one?"

The man looked up at the roof structure and slowly nodded. "Carpentry is what I learned many years ago. I certainly can help you."

"I can't pay you much, but I can offer you food and shelter in exchange for your work." She looked at him expectantly. Stan would be so pleased that they'd finally found someone to fix the roof – someone they could afford.

"It's a deal. Show me what needs to be done." He got up from the table and she led him to the second floor, where he scrutinized the remains of the roof structure. An hour later he entered the kitchen with a list of things he would need to get started.

"I'm sure we can get you most of this tomorrow in town. Stan will be so pleased."

"What will I be pleased about?" Stan came through the door smiling.

"Amos is going to repair the roof and—"

Stan's face fell as soon as he saw the other man and he

shot her a scathing stare. "Who's this Amos and what's his business in my house?"

It took Agnieska one glance into the darkness in Stan's eyes and the way he balled his hands into fists to know he was about to explode. Not wanting to make a scene in front of Amos, she walked past him and hissed, "Not here."

Stan trembled with suppressed rage and trailed after her into the vegetable garden. "Are you going to answer me?" he asked when she stopped and turned toward him.

"I am. Amos—"

"So you're on a firstname basis already." Stan stared at her with blatant fury.

"He's a survivor of the camps. Another Jew." She sighed and his glare softened a bit. "He came asking for water and then offered to work. Turns out he's a carpenter, and just what we needed."

"You had no right," Stan said, his jaw clenched. "Besides, we cannot afford to pay him. Or why do you think I haven't contracted with a carpenter in Lodz?"

"We don't need to pay him. He'll work for food and shelter."

"What kind of crazy woman are you? Inviting a stranger into the house? Where shall he sleep? With you under the staircase to keep you warm? Over my dead body!" Stan raised his voice with every word he said, but she wasn't afraid of him like she had been a decade earlier.

Despite being a grumpy, close-mouthed, savage man, she knew with certainty that no matter what kind of mood he was in, Stan would never lift a hand toward her. Emboldened by this knowledge she stepped up to him, rising to her full height of 5'5".

"Are you even listening to what you're saying? I won't tolerate such disrespect."

"I'm sorry." Stan deflated in front of her, seemingly shrinking down to her size, despite being half a foot taller than her. "But he cannot stay in the house. He has to leave."

"Look. This man is the answer to our prayers."

"I don't pray," he growled.

"But I do. And I believe Amos passed here for a reason. He could have stopped at any of the other farms to ask for water. Why here? Don't you think it's serendipity that he's a qualified carpenter? And a fellow Jew? He'll help us out fixing the roof we couldn't otherwise afford and we'll help him out with food and shelter."

Stan glared at her, but didn't utter a single word.

"This way you can work in the fields and the roof will still get repaired," she said, inhaling his musky scent. Even now, more furious than a bull in the arena, he was incredibly attractive and it took all her self-control not to reach out to touch his rough, calloused hand.

"Fine. But he won't sleep in the house, or anywhere near where he could hurt you," Stan finally said.

Agnieska nodded, thinking Stan was being ridiculous, but careful not to push him any more than she already had.

"Where do you suggest he sleep, if not in the house?" she asked, holding Stan's gaze.

"In the shed."

She raised a brow. "Then where will you sleep?"

"I'll bed down in the kitchen. That way he has to get past me if he does have any bad intentions."

"As you wish," she said, biting back the sharp response on her tongue. While a part of her appreciated his protectiveness, she wanted to tell him that she'd been successfully fending off unwanted advances for the last six years. "Dinner will be ready in a short while, so maybe you could go over the list of materials with Amos in the meanwhile."

Stan glared at her, but nodded and walked inside the house.

She stayed in the garden, picking tomatoes, bell peppers and a salad for dinner and then returned to the house. On the porch she listened for a moment, but the two men seemed to be civil to each other, because she didn't hear fighting or shouting.

CHAPTER 13

Stan entered the house, eyeing his possible rival with suspicion. This ruffian wasn't nearly good enough for Agnieska. She deserved so much better.

"So, you're Amos the carpenter? I'm Stan and this is my house."

"Your sister-in-law already told me so, and I'm grateful for the opportunity the two of you are giving me," Amos said, eying Stan with equal suspicion.

"Agnieska is a decent woman and I promise you, you'll wish yourself back into a Nazi camp if you ever lay a hand on her." Stan had no intention of beating around the bush. This intruder had to know exactly where he stood regarding the beautiful woman in this house. "Understood?"

"I hear you loud and clear."

"Then let me show you where you can sleep," Stan said and led Amos from the house, just as Agnieska returned from the garden. She'd taken on a healthy tan from being outside a lot and had gained at least ten pounds since she'd arrived at his doorstep all skin and bones. The roundness of her hips, shoulders, and face made her all the more attractive. Even her wonderful breasts looked fuller and the slightest glance at them made his blood rush south. She smiled at both of the men, sending a stabbing pain of jealousy deep into Stan's heart.

"Here's the shed. I hope this is good enough for you." Stan pointed at the mattress and blanket lying on the plain floor.

"Thank you. I've had worse." Amos put down his small bundle of things.

For a short moment, guilt filled Stan's mind. This man had endured so much at the hands of the Nazis. But that didn't justify letting down his guard against the stranger. Not where Agnieska was concerned.

"If you need anything, let me know," he said, half appeased. "You can wash over there at the well. We have a wooden barrel, but only cold water."

"That'll do. I don't need much. And thank you again for your kindness."

I'm not kind. I wish you'd leave sooner rather than later, because I don't want you anywhere near her. "Dinner is almost ready. Don't be late." After the orders, Stan turned and left the shed. Begrudgingly, he had to admit that Amos was a living, breathing example of everything Stan was not. He had two functional legs and was much more suited to providing for her in the long term. Given the fact that Amos was also a Jew just like her, he was the obvious choice.

As much as Stan believed Agnieska deserved better than

himself, now that an actual prospect had appeared, he rather wished for her to die an old spinster.

Dinner was an awkward affair, with Agnieska trying to make conversation and both men avoiding talking to each other. Stan fled the table as soon as he finished eating, glad he had the excuse to visit Tadzio's house and ask them to borrow a blanket.

When he returned, Amos had retreated to the shed and Agnieska was fast asleep in her alcove. He looked at her, so tiny and yet so strong. A smile spread across his face as he remembered how the fearless woman had put him in his place earlier today. Not that he would ever tell her, but that kind of behavior endeared her even more to him.

He turned away. Sadly, she'd never be his. But she wouldn't be Amos' either – not if he had a say.

Sleeping on the kitchen floor with nothing but the blanket Malgorzata had loaned him was uncomfortable to say the least, but he slept with a smile on his face, knowing the first thing he'd see in the morning would be Agnieska's sweet face.

Throughout the next days, he went out of his way to find little jobs that needed to be done right away. Jobs that kept him close to the house where he could not only watch over Agnieska, but also make sure Amos didn't step out of line.

On the third day, Agnieska grew tired of his behavior and confronted him.

"What are you doing?" She was standing at the side of the garden, her hands on her hips and a hard look in her eyes.

He set the piece of wood down and stared back at her.

"What do you mean, what am I doing? I'm getting the wood prepared for the fence you want put up around the house."

Stan wasn't quite sure what to do with Agnieska when she was confronting him. No girl or woman apart from his mother and younger sister had ever dared. Usually one intimidating look and a raising of his voice was enough to end an argument. But not with her. Her courage exasperated as well as excited him. *God, she's gorgeous when she's pissed off! I wonder how she'll behave when making love.*

The thought of her hoarse voice, heavy with passion as it commanded him to pleasure her, sent hot waves down south and all he could do was pray she didn't notice the growing bulge in his worker's blues. So far most of his interactions of the sexual variety had been hushed encounters behind his grandparents' barn as a youth, and later in the woods with the harlots traveling with the partisans.

But that had been before the amputation of his leg. Before he'd sworn off intimacy, women, and love for the remainder of his miserable life. And long before he'd fallen in love with Agnieska. With her it would be a celebration of love, passion and life itself. With her, he'd take all the time in the world to make it an outstanding experience for both of them.

If only…

"Are you listening to me?" Agnieska asked loudly.

Obviously he had no idea what she'd been saying, but he wasn't to let her know. "I'm listening all right, but the real question should be what gives you the right to challenge what I do?"

"If you're wasting precious time with unimportant work—"

"Unimportant? And since when do you get to decide what is important around here? This is my house. I give the orders, not you."

Agnieska looked at him and folded her arms across her chest, drawing his eyes to her pushed up breasts. "You want to say that again? Let me make one thing clear: I don't take orders from you."

The words tumbled out of his mouth before he could stop them. "This is my farm. I'm the boss. And you better do as I say." One glimpse into her eyes, where a hard glint took up residence, told him he'd made a mistake.

"If you truly feel that way, it probably is time for me to leave." She squared her shoulders and took a deep breath. "For six long years I've been forced to obey every rule, carry out every cruel order the Nazis gave me. I'm done with obeying. I'm not letting anyone do this to me again."

"Please, you don't have to leave," Stan begged her, realizing she was serious about her threat.

"Well, that's not what I'm hearing. Either I get to have a say in things around here or I'm gone."

Fear gripped him, and he swallowed his anger and his pride. "I'm sorry." He paused for a long moment and finally admitted, "Maybe I've overreacted."

"You've been overreacting from the minute Amos arrived at the farm." Her voice softened but her eyes still showed her determination not to give in.

"Look, I admit, his arrival sent me off-kilter. But only because I'm trying to protect you. I've sworn an oath to myself that nobody will ever harm you again. Not on my watch. The small smile lighting up her face spurred him on.

"I apologize for being an ass and promise not to do it again. But please, don't leave. Please."

She stared at him for a moment longer and then nodded. "Good." Then she spun on her heel and stalked off.

Stan watched her go, feeling like the biggest brute in the world. He hated that Agnieska kept seeing him at his worst, but there was no way he could sit by and allow someone else to swoop in and snatch her away.

CHAPTER 14

Agnieska briskly walked down the road for close to an hour.

Away. Away. Away from the man who made her livid with his antics. What on earth had caused him to behave like a loose cannon since the day Amos arrived at the farm?

She'd believed he would be as pleased as she was to finally have found someone who could repair the roof. A carpenter, no less. And they didn't even have to pay him.

Didn't Stan see that the house would be permanently damaged if it had to withstand another winter without its roof? Didn't he know that they couldn't live there with the cold eastern winds sweeping inside night and day? Had he any idea how uninhabitable it would get once the heavy autumn storms brought rain and snow? Did he really want to stay in the flimsy shed throughout the winter?

Despite his words that he wasn't attracted to her, he behaved very much like he owned her. She wrinkled her nose. His possessiveness had been cute, but since Amos arrived at the farm, Stan had gone too far. After being reduced to a spineless subhuman puppet for such a long time, she'd be damned before she allowed anyone to dominate her ever again.

Even well-meaning Stan.

It was his house, all right. But it was her work, sweat and effort that had turned it into a home again. So far he'd left her to do as she pleased with everything concerning the house and the garden.

Why did he now pester her, trying to control her every step? Inventing excuses to stick around the house all day? Had she done something wrong? Was he really still furious that she'd taken the liberty of hiring a carpenter for the roof?

I thought he'd be delighted. I thought he wanted us to have a cozy home this winter.

She shook her head; there was nothing transparent or comprehensible about his behavior. After another fifteen minutes of brisk walking she turned onto another road leading in a circle back to the farm. Her anger slowly dissolved, but what stayed was a deep sadness.

Without noticing it, she'd walked all the way back and was approaching Tadzio's house just when Malgorzata came outside to take down the dry laundry.

"Hello, Agnieska, have you been to town?"

"No, just taking a walk," she said.

"A walk?" Malgorzata laughed. Talking a walk wasn't something a farmwoman did, because where should she find the time to indulge in leisure? "If you're taking a walk, something must be awfully wrong. Come inside and have a tea with me."

Agnieska glanced at Tadzio's mother and then into the distance at Stan's farm. It was tempting to talk to a more experienced woman. Maybe she had an explanation for Stan's unnerving behavior.

"Tadzio told me you found someone to fix the roof."

"Yes, he's a survivor from the camps and offered to work in exchange for food and shelter." Agnieska sipped the hot, aromatic sage infusion.

"It was about time. Not long before the autumn storms arrive," Malgorzata said with a frown.

"I know there's so much to do still. And Stan keeps saying that we need at least two more weeks of sunshine for the harvest…."

Malgorzata gave her a scrutinizing stare, but didn't say a word.

"Where are your children?"

"Tadzio has taken Lola into the woods to collect mushrooms. We're alone," Malgorzata said, sipping her tea. "Now, tell me what has you so upset."

"It's just… Stan is behaving so unreasonably. He keeps doing tasks near the house instead of staying in the fields like he used to. I'm worried we won't have enough food for the winter."

"What else are you worried about?" Malgorzata's blue eyes seemed to know the truth already and somehow this gave Agnieska the courage to speak out loud.

"Stan. He's changed. He's become brooding, tight-lipped and short-tempered."

"Isn't that the Stanislaw we all know and fear?"

Agnieska sighed. "When he was younger, yes. But since I

arrived on the farm, he's been different. Considerate, kind, protective."

"Protective? Of you?"

"Yes."

Malgorzata laughed out loud. "That explains everything!"

Agnieska stared at the other woman with wide eyes, without the slightest idea what she was talking about.

"He's jealous."

"Jealous? Stan? But why?" Agnieska was even more confused.

"Because this carpenter watches you with interest no matter where you go. Stan is afraid he'll make a move on you."

"On me?" Agnieska was perplexed. Amos had never shown any attention toward her apart from the necessary interactions, and even then he always maintained his distance. He wasn't even friendly with her, merely businesslike. And Stan being jealous? Hadn't he made it clear that there could never be more than friendship between them?

"Oh, yes. This carpenter, he's watching you like a hawk, with that yearning in his eyes when a man watches the woman he wants."

"I had no idea..." Agnieska shook her head. She was in this way over her head.

Malgorzata patted her arm. "No need to worry. It's better to have two admirers than one."

"Two?" Agnieska's brain had gone numb, with all the new information Malgorzata presented. Could this be true?

"I told you before that Stanislaw fancied you—"

"That was Jarek," Agnieska interrupted her.

For a moment the other woman looked confused, but then shrugged her shoulders. "Never could tell them apart. But what I see now is that our Stanislaw has it bad for you. And that makes a man act without thought or reason. Now it's up to you to decide which of the men you wish to encourage."

Agnieska's heart raced and a heated blush rose to her cheeks. The answer was easy. "I find Stan quite attractive." The heat intensified as the image of his bare back came to her mind. Slim hips. Broad shoulders. Strong muscles. Tan skin. Even the scars on his back enhanced his gorgeousness. As if to dispel suspicion about her train of thoughts, she added, "I mean his personality as much as his physique."

Malgorzata laughed. "He definitely is a handsome lad, even with his missing leg. And I can tell you, more than one woman in town would be licking her fingers if she could have a roll in the hay with him."

Tingling heat attacked all Agnieska's senses. It was such a scandalous, yet strangely exciting, image to have a roll in the hay with Stan.

"I see, you like to entertain this idea," Malgorzata giggled.

"He told me there can never be anything but friendship between us."

"Oh, did he?" Malgorzata raised a brow. "And why would that be?"

"Because... because he thinks I deserve better." *Because he feels he's not a real man anymore.*

"Well, that nonsense is just another clear sign that he's

fallen head over heels for you. Now you just have to encourage him to take the first step."

Realization trickled into Agnieska's bones and suddenly his erratic actions made sense. She wanted to shake the stupid pride out of him, and tell him how things really worked. That she didn't want anyone else but him.

"Now go and make sure Stanislaw knows you're not interested in that other man. He'll come around in time. He needs a strong woman like you in his life. He is not good at being alone."

On her way back to the farm, Agnieska fluctuated between being angry with him and wanting him to wrap her in his arms and kiss her again.

CHAPTER 15

By the time she reached the farmhouse the sun was already low on the horizon. It cast a golden light across the fields and for a moment she saw the yellow sheaves bowing their heavy heads in the breeze like it used to be all those years ago. She blinked and the image evaporated, the fields lay barren, except for the green patches Stan and Tadzio had planted in a Herculean effort to beat time.

The air was still warm, but it smelled of rain, cool nights and the end of summer. It was the season to pick blackberries, mushrooms, and hunt deer. She would have to ask Malgorzata how to salt meat to keep it for winter. If – if Stan would even be able to go hunting. All Poles had been ordered to turn in their weapons to the new authorities, but she knew that Stan kept a rifle hidden in the shed. Well, maybe not in the shed anymore, since Amos had taken up his quarters there.

Her mind drifted from the carpenter's friendly person to Stan's grumpy self. Others would probably tell her to have her head examined, but she preferred the boisterous, moody, brooding man with a wooden leg a hundred times over the quiet, kind and soft-spoken Amos. Just how should she encourage bull-headed Stan to take the first step like Malgorzata had suggested?

When she rounded the corner she all but bumped into Stan, whose resulting scowl could frighten a scarecrow.

"There you are! I was worried about you."

"I was walking off my anger at you." She didn't want to mention her visit with Malgorzata for fear he might ask her, what the two women had been talking about. She wouldn't be able to lie to him, but she couldn't very well tell him what Tadzio's mother had suggested, either.

"I guess I deserved that," he said, his striking blue eyes settling on her. Unsettling her. The guilty look on his face didn't take an ounce away from his attractiveness, and she squirmed under his scrutinizing gaze.

"Probably," she said, ducking her head and walking around him into the kitchen. But he followed her like a puppy and flopped onto one of the chairs, boring his stare into her back. It was unnerving.

"What do you want?" she finally snapped and turned around to glare at him. The man sitting across her looked like a drowned rat and the guilty look on his face endeared him even more to her.

"We need to talk," he said and gestured at the chair opposite him. "Please?"

She nodded, smoothed her hands down her dress and

walked over to where he sat with her heart racing. Would he tell her to leave? She didn't want to leave. Despite his mood swings she couldn't imagine being without him by her side.

Since she'd appeared on his doorsteps two months earlier, she'd grown accustomed to having him around. Talking to him. Joking with him. Laughing with him. He always made sure she had everything she needed and she hadn't felt as safe in years as she did in his presence. The only drawback was the times when he acted like a jealous ass… she bit on her lips to prevent herself from laughing. How could he even suspect that she favored a bland man like Amos?

As soon as she settled on the chair, he started to talk. "I'm so sorry… I had no right to talk to you the way I did… I'm so angry. Disillusioned. Sometimes it overwhelms me and I explode. But you know I would never hurt you, right?"

"I know this, but…"

"But? Are you afraid of me?" he asked, his agitation visible in the contorted expression of his face.

"No." She smiled. "I used to be afraid of you when we were young. Everyone was. You had quite the reputation." His embarrassed expression was priceless. "But that was a long time ago. We're both grownups now and we've gone through ordeals nobody should have to experience." She stopped, a shudder racking her shoulders.

"If I could make it all up to you, I would." His wonderful blue eyes softened, caressing her, showering her with tenderness.

"I know you would, and believe me, you're the reason

why I have never been happier in my life, despite the awful things that happened."

"Really?" He beamed with delight, taking her hand between his huge paws. She loved the rough scratch of his callouses on her skin, wishing for nothing more than being wrapped up in his arms forever.

"Really," she answered. "It doesn't mean that I'm not sad, angry, hurt, and damaged from what happened. But the past is part of what defines us and what formed us into becoming the persons we are now. I, for my part, want to focus on the present, and a brighter future."

"Agnieska, I... you're a much better person than I am. You have such a gentle spirit, that even the Nazis couldn't crush. I promise I'm going to control my temper better from now on."

"I don't even understand what set you off," she said. "I believed you'd love the fact that we found someone to repair the roof before winter."

A shadow fell across his face. "You're right. I ought to be delighted, but, the moment I first saw Amos, I was afraid he'd steal you away from me."

Malgorzata was right! Agnieska widened her eyes in shock. "You're acting like this because you're jealous?"

"I'm afraid so. Remember I told you there can't be anything between us but friendship?"

She nodded. Of course she remembered. How could she not remember the single most hurtful words he'd ever said to her?

"I lied."

"You lied? Why?" she gasped, hot shots of longing coursing through her veins.

"Because I want only the best for you, and I'm not the best you can have." After the critical words, he looked so sad that it slashed her heart.

"Do I get a say in what is good for me?" She tried a small smile, wanting him to stop being so stubborn and just take her into his arms.

"If you insist…" Stan bent forward and leveled his bright blue eyes with hers. Suddenly the world stopped spinning and Agnieska jumped deep into the soul that lay hidden beneath those eyes. She had no idea how and when, but when reality reminded her of its existence, she was in his arms, pressed against his hard chest.

"I want to kiss you," he whispered into her ear.

Agnieska's eyes widened, stupefied. She raised her head to look at him and the tenderness in his eyes was all she needed to reply, "Yes. Kiss me."

Stan raised one hand, threading his fingers through the hair at her nape and angling her head for his possession. Ever so slowly his lips came down, hovering over hers for a moment, before they finally landed on her mouth. The tender touch electrified her, sending hot shivers racing through her.

She wondered what she was expected to do, but the wetness of his tongue tracing her lips scrambled her wits and would turn her into a blubbering, moaning mess in another second. His mouth moved away from hers to place little kisses across her cheek, giving her the time to recover from the sensual attack.

Panic rose in her. "Wait, Stan."

"What, sweetheart?" His mouth had reached her earlobe

and nibbled at it, sending the butterflies in her stomach into frenzy.

"Don't stop kissing me just yet," she whispered. Surprised by her boldness, she quickly closed her eyes, hoping he hadn't heard. But no such luck.

Stan gave a low, growling chuckle. "At your service, ma'am," he murmured, kissing his way back to her mouth. His hands held her still, but she was desperate to get closer to him, soak up his heat, and feel the strength of his body.

A moan escaped her throat, which seemed to spur him on, because he intensified the pressure on her lips and she parted them for him. This time she was prepared to receive his tongue, and the intense pleasure silenced the nagging voice in her head saying that a decent woman didn't behave like this.

His tongue delved deeper, flooding her nerve endings with sensations she'd never felt before. The tingling his exploring tongue caused in her mouth rolled all the way down to her toes, before it pooled deep between her legs.

If it weren't for his big hands holding her tight, her legs would have given out beneath her. Never had she felt so weak before. Never had she felt so good before. Never had she been kissed like this. Electricity flowed with every lap of his tongue, shooting straight to her core and making her shiver with an unfamiliar need.

He seemed equally affected, grinding his pelvis against her as his tongue thrust into her mouth, mimicking what he wanted to do with other parts of his. Agnieska's brain went blissfully blank and she surrendered to the sensations he created, ignoring the little frisson of fear that urged her to pull away from him.

Strength. Determination. Need. Love. It was all there in his kiss. He tasted her with his tongue and teeth, exploring her mouth with abandon while she all but melted in his arms. Her hands clutched him tightly and when he moved she discovered that she had wedged one thigh between his own without even realizing she'd been seeking more of his touch.

Stan broke away from her mouth with a groan and spun them both around until her back was pressed up against the closest structure, the back wall of the staircase. He held her captive with his hot body, his lips returning to hers and both of his hands cupping her neck.

She moaned into his mouth, her hands clutching his shoulders as she held on for the sensual ride. There was so much feeling in a simple kiss; she feared she'd faint into his arms if he continued the assault on her senses.

The sound of Amos clearing his throat tore Agnieska from her blissful state and she pulled her head away from Stan's kiss so hard that she banged it on the wall behind her. Stan released her, breathing heavily and looking like he wanted to commit murder over the intrusion.

She dropped her eyes, embarrassment at having been surprised in such a delicate position making her cheeks and ears burn.

"Stop looking like the world just ended. We didn't do anything wrong," Stan whispered, shielding her from Amos's view with his broad body. She was thankful for the time Stan gave her to compose herself and straighten the wrinkles in her skirt. But how would she ever be able to look Amos in the eye again, after he'd seen her acting like a veritable harlot? Agnieska straightened her spine before stepping out from behind Stan's back.

"I'm sorry. I thought I heard noises," Amos said, apparently as embarrassed as she was.

"Dinner will be ready in ten minutes," Agnieska replied, pretending nothing had happened.

CHAPTER 16

Stan wasn't ashamed of kissing Agnieska, but one glance at her told him that *she* was deeply embarrassed having been caught red-handed. So he decided to usher Amos out of the kitchen to give her the opportunity to compose herself.

"Could you lend me a hand outside?" Stan asked him.

"Sure," Amos said, but the disapproving glint in his eyes belied his answer.

Stan walked out with his rival on his heels. The distress of dashed hopes rolled off of Amos in waves and Stan almost felt sorry for him. He'd always sensed that Amos had set his sights on Agnieska. Understandably. But he wouldn't get her. Not as long as Stan had a say in the matter.

His heart rejoiced as he remembered the kiss. Where kisses were concerned, this one had knocked the breath out of him, and he didn't dare imagine what would have happened if they hadn't been interrupted.

Once again he reminded himself that he needed to take

it slow with Agnieska. She wasn't an easy woman. And he sure as hell didn't want to scare her or make her regret anything.

"What did you need help with?" Amos asked, leaving Stan flustered for a moment.

"Ah..." His glance fell on a piece of wood he'd been polishing to make shelves. "I can't carry this up to the porch by myself."

Amos gave him an unbelieving look, because he'd seen Stan carry heavier things. But he helped without another word.

"Dinner is ready," Agnieska called from the kitchen.

"I'll eat later. I need to finish some work on the roof before darkness settles," Amos said.

"Sure, man. I'll tell her to keep your meal warm." Stan gave a deep and satisfied sigh when Amos disappeared around the corner of the house. The man had understood the message. He wouldn't dare make a move on Stan's woman.

The next morning Stan woke as someone snuck into the kitchen where he slept. He squeezed open one eye in the incomprehensible hope it was Agnieska coming to repeat their kiss. But to his disappointment it was Amos, cutting a few slices of bread and stuffing them into his shoulder bag.

What the hell? Stan opened both eyes, and asked, "What are you doing?"

"I've stayed too long as it is. I need to get moving or I

won't reach my destination before the weather turns," Amos answered.

Stan heard his words and saw them for the excuse they were. It wouldn't do any good to humiliate the man, so he got up, handed him a bag of potatoes and said, "Safe travels."

"Thanks… and take care of her." Amos stepped outside and walked toward the road.

"What just happened in here?" Agnieska entered the kitchen, a suspicious look on her face.

"Nothing."

"Nothing?"

"Amos left."

"He… did what?"

Stan took a step toward her, pressing a soft kiss to her cheek. She melted into his arms and he couldn't care less what Amos did or said. But the peace only lasted a few moments, before she pushed out of his embrace and gave him a stern look. "Did you have anything to do with his sudden departure?"

"No. Cross my heart and hope to die." He made the motion in the center of his chest.

She giggled and slapped his shoulder. "You'd better not get caught breaking that oath."

"You have known me long enough to know that I never break a promise."

"I have." Her deep pools of green locked with his and a warm feeling spread from his heart into his entire body. A crazy desire followed the warmth, urging him to rip the clothes off of her and expose her to his gaze. Only a thin thread of self-control remained, when she melted against him, her head leaning into his shoulder.

The fresh scent of her hair tested his restraint and all he could do was hold her tight, pressing little kisses onto her head.

"Woman, you'd better take a step back or I can't be held responsible for my actions," he groaned.

Agnieska jumped out of his arms. "Are you serious?"

He opened his mouth to chuckle, but the terror in her eyes kept him from doing so. "I'm sorry, sweetheart, if I frightened you. I desire you so much; more than I thought was humanly possible. But while I certainly am dying to make love to you, I'd never do anything you don't want to."

She nodded, somehow reassured.

"Do you trust me?" he asked, suddenly afraid she might run away.

She nodded again.

"I need you to say it, Agnieska. Say the words. Tell me that you trust me never to take anything you aren't willingly giving me."

Finally she smiled. "I trust you, Stan. I trust that you won't do anything I don't want."

"Goodness. Woman. You're slaying me here," he said. As much as he wanted to keep holding her, kissing her, laughing with her, there were more pressing issues at the moment. "Let's have a look at the roof before we eat breakfast," he said.

Together, they climbed the stairs. To the left side was the master bedroom that had belonged to his grandparents and then to his parents. They ventured inside and saw that the roof was finished, except for a few small details.

"That looks quite good," Agnieska said.

"Yes, let's have a look at the rooms on the other side." On

the right side of the stairs were two smaller rooms. He opened the door to the first room and gaped up into an open hole. His jaw tightened as he took stock of the situation. As far as he could see, about half of the roof on this side of the house was completed.

"Well, that doesn't look quite as good," Agnieska murmured, looking up at the unfinished roof.

"It sure doesn't," he said. For a moment he wished Amos had stayed longer. "We can't leave it like it is. Not with winter just a few months away."

"We'll find someone else to help us." She leaned against him, wrapping his arm around her shoulder. "Amos did all the heavy work with the supporting beams, it's just putting the roofing tiles in place. Anyone can do that part."

"Not me." His entire body tensed at the reminder of his disability and he involuntarily squeezed her tighter, afraid she might finally comprehend what he'd known all along: that he wasn't good enough for her.

"Me, neither," she said, turning around in his arms and locking eyes with him.

"You're not a man."

"What makes you think that every man has to be able to fix a roof?" she said, her eyes taking on a challenging glint.

Of course she was right. But he *wanted* to be able to do it. Worse yet, he'd been perfectly capable only a year prior.

"I like you just the way you are," she said in a soft voice, taking away all his sorrows and his feelings of inadequacy.

"I want you to move into the master bedroom," he said.

"And what about you?"

"I can sleep in the shed for a while longer." It was late

September and the nights were still warm, but that would change in the coming weeks.

She smiled at him. "I'll move up here, but under one condition. If the roof isn't ready by the time we're getting the first nightly frost, I'll return to the alcove beneath the stairs and you sleep here."

"It's a deal," he said, secretly hoping that by then he would have her convinced to share the room – and the bed – with him.

"Why don't you go to work with Tadzio and I'll ask Malgorzata and Old Jakub to help me carry the closet and the new bed upstairs," she said, referring to the furniture they'd been buying and making for the upper rooms and storing in the hallway.

He knew what she was doing. Sparing him from the embarrassment of not being able to help. But for once he didn't argue with her. "Yes, ma'am."

Her happy giggle was reward enough.

After another day of hard work he returned from the fields to a woman giddy with pleasure.

"Stan, you have to have a look. It's wonderful!" She propelled him up the stairs and showed him her new realm, where he kissed her on the cheek.

Clapping hands caused him to turn his head and find Malgorzata and her daughter Lola watching.

"Thanks for your help. I think we should open a bottle of vodka and celebrate."

They all adjourned downstairs and while Tadzio and his little sister played outside, the three adults toasted one another and the new start Stan and Agnieska were making in rebuilding his parents' house.

"This is good," Malgorzata said after they'd emptied the bottle together. "But I should get my children home and let you continue this celebration without us." She winked at Agnieska before leaving the room.

"Are you happy?" he asked Agnieska.

"I'm delirious," she answered. "Thank you for everything."

He wrapped an arm around her shoulders and pressed a kiss on her lips. Heat rushed into his groin. Her soft curves pressed against him and needy moans escaped her throat, making him want more. Much more. But the alcohol swirled in his veins and he knew he wouldn't be able to control himself in his current state.

With a deep sigh he pulled away after kissing her one last time. "I'd better leave now. I'm not sure I can trust myself enough after all the vodka we had."

"I'll see you tomorrow. Thank you for watching out for me," she said and turned to climb the stairs.

His heart exploded with love.

CHAPTER 17

Agnieska lay in her bed, if she wasn't hovering inches above the mattress, feeling happier than she had in a long time. He'd been so kind and sweet today. And his kisses… she touched her swollen lips, still tingling with desire.

It had been a disappointment when he'd left her yearning for more. But at the same time she was relieved. Nobody had taken the time to explain to her what really happened when a man and a woman lay together, but judging by the grave expressions of the older women, it was a painful and annoying affair. Something a woman had to endure, just like scrubbing clothes all day with raw fingers.

Although… her dearest sister Ludmila, who'd married Stan's brother Peter, never seemed to dread the nights spent with her husband. Ludmila never talked about what happened between the sheets, but Agnieska could tell from the rosy flush on her cheeks in the morning that she thoroughly enjoyed whatever her husband did to her.

Maybe it wasn't all that bad?

The one thing she was sure about, was that she was falling in love with Stan a little bit more each day, and she couldn't imagine ever living without him again.

The cock-a-doodle-doo woke her early in the morning to the twilight filtering through the lattice-blinds painted peculiar patterns on the wall. She smiled, following the lines of light and shadow with her eyes, until she paused. There was an odd fracture in the pattern. She got up, gliding her hand across the wall until she felt it: a distinct edge.

Frantically she tore the wallpaper away and found a hidden door, the size of a small suitcase. Her fingers trembling and her heart pounding against her ribs, she felt around the edges of the door, until she found the push mechanism to open the door.

A shudder of guilt ran down her spine. Was she prying into someone's life? Should she ask Stan to come up and have a look? But curiosity prevailed and she opened the door wide. Behind it was a space in the wall, about as deep as a hand and twenty inches wide and high.

It contained two small metal boxes. She took them out and sat on the bed, oblivious to her surroundings. The first box contained the wedding bands of Stan's parents, a golden brooch, a small golden cross and a blue garter made of the finest lace. She fingered the aged material, wondering to whom it had belonged. Then she returned everything to the box and opened the second one.

It was full to the brim with photographs. A stern looking couple she didn't recognize on their wedding day, probably Stan's grandparents. Several pictures of Stan's parents with their four children. She was about to return them to the box, ashamed at prying into things that weren't hers, when her glance fell on the photograph of a beautiful young woman with black hair, high cheekbones and the happiest smile on her face, holding the hand of a handsome young man.

Tears sprung to her eyes as she traced her fingers across the woman in the picture, who wore the most beautiful wedding dress. *Ludmila. My beloved sister.* She remembered it like yesterday when her six-year-older sister had told their parents that she was in the family way. They'd been upset, enraged even. But Peter had convinced them to let her marry him. He'd even offered to move to Warsaw, away from his family, so Ludmila could finish her education. It had been an emergency wedding, but nevertheless it had been so beautiful. And both Ludmila and Peter seemed so happy.

More tears flowed down Agnieska's face. Ludmila was dead. Her parents were dead. Her grandparents. Her aunts and uncles. Her cousins. Her friends.

Dead.

Dead.

Dead.

The tears flowed freely. She slid down the bed, sinking to the floor, sobs wracking her body. She rocked back and forth, clutching the picture to her chest as tears streamed down her face. The carefully hidden pain surfaced, attacking her with the force of a grenade, shattering her heart into a million pieces.

She sniffed and sobbed, cried and howled, wishing herself away from the pain. What right did she have to ever be happy again, when so many others couldn't? It wasn't fair that she'd survived, when she wasn't any better than them.

Mired in her grief, she was oblivious to her surroundings. Didn't notice the time passing, or Stan call her name. She didn't even hear the door open when he came inside, muttering a curse when he found her in her desolate state of mind.

He put a hand on her shoulder and she started, an irrational fear filling her chest.

"What's wrong?" he asked, concern etched on his face.

Agnieska looked up at him, the fear fading away even as the deep sorrow she felt consumed her. She couldn't answer him, couldn't utter a single word and sobbed all the harder under his scrutinizing gaze. He reached out and pried the photograph out of her hands, staring at it for a long moment.

She cleared her throat several times, trying to find her voice as more tears streamed down her cheeks. He laid the photograph on the bed and slid to the floor, sitting beside her and wrapping his arms around her, pulling her in close. Agnieska closed her eyes and gave herself over to the comfort he offered. She knew she should be stronger, but just for a little while she wanted to relinquish all her grief, anger, and guilt.

Stan was there, offering her comfort and warmth. Another human being who knew the depths of hell she'd crossed to come out on the other side. Not unscathed, but alive. He didn't need words to convey that he understood – understood her struggle with all these emotions. The same emotions he struggled with day after day and that made him burst into fits of rage more often than not. Neither of them moved. Even long after her tears abated, she continued to stay in his arms, allowing her heartbreak free rein.

"Where did you find that photograph?" he finally asked her.

The reality hit her again square in the chest. The injustice, that his brother Peter was still alive while her sister Ludmila had died, fueled the hatred in her heart and moments later, she couldn't hold back the rage. Hatred, fury, desolation and grief spilled out of her.

Raising her fists, she pummeled them into his chest. Seemingly shocked at her outburst, he caught her wrists, holding them tight.

"Don't you dare touch me!" she screamed at him, trying to free herself from his grip.

"Calm down, will you please?" Stan said, still holding her in his iron grip, which only caused her to double the intensity of her struggle.

Guilt over her lone survival and shame for wanting to be happy with him added to the volatile cocktail of emotions, and she sagged, only to tear her wrists from his hands when she felt him loosen his grip. The next moment, she pummeled into him again and this time he didn't try to stop her.

"Damn you! Damn you for making me feel again! I should have died in the Nazi camps. Why did I survive and everyone else didn't? How dare you make me believe I could ever be happy again! I don't deserve it. I don't."

Throughout her tirade, Stan sat there stoically, taking her abuse and murmuring words meant to comfort her. They only served to increase her need to hurt him as much as she was hurting deep inside.

CHAPTER 18

Stan felt utterly helpless. All he could do was hold her throughout her emotional breakdown, murmuring words of comfort and letting her take out her rage on him, because nothing seemed to be penetrating the darkness that consumed her.

"Agnieska, you need to breathe, sweetheart. Calm down and talk to me." When she still didn't react, he tightened his arms around her, bringing her flush against him. She struggled and writhed against him.

The next moment she thrashed her entire lightweight body against him and more out of surprise than from the actual impact, he toppled over, taking her with him to the floor. He rolled over onto his good side and came to lie half on top of her, grabbing her hands and pinning them above her head. She seared him with a scathing stare, unabated fury still raging within her.

"I need you to calm down," he said, not wavering from her stare until he noticed a shift in her mood. Her body softened and she stopped struggling against him. He released her hands and she wrapped them around his shoulders even as she said, "Kiss me, Stan. Show me there's something worth living for."

He wanted to say no. Wanted to move away from her – but how could he deny her begging eyes? It was just a kiss. Nothing more. As soon as he pressed his lips onto hers and she thrust her tongue into his mouth he knew he would never be able to stop.

"Sweetheart, are you sure this is what you want?" he hissed.

"Must. Need. Must feel alive. Please, don't go," she stammered.

"Let us at least get onto the bed," he said. If she had second thoughts, this was her chance to make him stop, otherwise... Agnieska did nothing more but gaze with her big green eyes, setting every cell inside him on fire. Somehow she helped him up and they stumbled onto the bed.

CHAPTER 19

Stan woke, slightly disoriented, from a ray of sunshine tickling his nose. He opened his eyes, blinking several times as he tried to recall where he was. Judging by the position of the sun it was way past noon and he should have been up and working for hours... then it all came rushing back. The lovemaking with Agnieska.

He reached out a hand, expecting to encounter her warm body. But the other side of the bed was empty, and the sheets were cool to his touch. She wasn't there. She hadn't been there for quite some time.

Obviously she wasn't a slouch like him, sleeping all morning. He listened for her moving around downstairs, but he heard nothing. He lay back for a moment, allowing memories of the events before to bring a smile to his face.

It had been more than just the physical connection; it had been a meeting of their souls. Extra Special. Stan had never felt this way before. Like he belonged – to her.

A noise downstairs alerted him that she was back in the

house. He quickly donned his shirt, adjusted and buttoned up his trousers and headed down the stairs. His stomach protested the long fasting, since he'd skipped breakfast this morning, and he hoped Agnieska was preparing lunch for them. A smile crossed his face, even as he imagined wrapping her into his arms from behind.

When he entered the kitchen, however, Agnieska was nowhere to be found. The level of disappointment he felt took him by surprise. He looked about the kitchen, noticing right away that the huge basket she used when visiting the market was missing. It wasn't her normal day to visit the town, though.

He saw the lunch stew in a thermos on the table, several pieces of bread on a plate. Another smile spread across his face, as he greedily opened the thermos bowl to smell the food. Potato stew with meat and carrots. Despite his hunger, the meal wouldn't taste as good as usual. It just wasn't the same without her to share it with him.

Putting the dirty dishes into the sink, he wondered where she'd gone and when she'd be back, when the back door smashed open.

"Hey, here you are! I've been waiting for you all morning." Tadzio rushed in, exuberant and talkative.

"I'm sorry, but I'm ready now." Stan wasn't going to tell the boy why he hadn't been in the fields. They walked together in silence to the far end of the one field they'd managed to plant earlier this summer.

"We should harvest the cabbage before it gets too cold at night," Stan said.

Tadzio nodded gravely, pretending he knew all about farming. "Will we have enough food for the winter?"

"I sure hope so. But since we couldn't sow crops and planted everything late, we have to pray the weather will be warm for another two weeks at least."

"My mom says we'll get frost any day now." Tadzio bent down to pull out a carrot. A rather small carrot.

"That's what I'm worried about. Most of the vegetables will survive a few degrees beneath freezing point, but not more."

They worked on pulling out weeds and watering the plants, but worry stayed uppermost in Stan's mind. After six long years the war was finally over, but now the country faced a whole slew of other problems. The armies had left devastation in their wake, and since Germany hadn't capitulated until mid-May, the stream of returning soldiers, slave laborers and concentration camp inmates hadn't even fully started until June.

Much too late for properly tending to the farms. Everywhere in Poland fields lay barren, unable to nurture the population. If winter came early, that would only decrease the already meager harvest. Stan could already see a famine sweeping his beloved country.

But it wasn't just food that had him concerned. There were worrisome rumors ravaging the nation. The struggle for power in the void left behind by the Nazis was over – and the Communists had won. Supported by Stalin and his Red Army they were assuming control of the country.

Their way of ridding themselves of the opposition was so eerily similar to the means the Nazis had used, it was scary. Throngs of people were sent to Siberia to "re-education camps", others disappeared or perished in the basements of the NKVD prisons – surely by the same means the

Gestapo had taken. He scoffed. Personally he thought Poland had replaced one evil with another. And their so-called Allies, Great Britain and America, had sold them out to the Soviet Union even before the war had ended.

He balled his hands into fists. Would the suffering never end? Would he live to see the day when Poland was truly free again? It was a difficult time and Stan feared it was only going to get worse. Not better. He feared for their safety and their future. Most of all, he feared his inability to protect Agnieska if things got bad again.

He returned to the house that evening. Looking forward to seeing Agnieska, he washed up at the pump outside before he walked into the kitchen. With a broad grin he wrapped his arm around her shoulders, but she shrugged him off and stepped to the side.

Stan gave her a frown. "What's wrong?" he asked her.

"Nothing's wrong. I have to make dinner." She refused to turn around and after watching her for several long moments, Stan gave her what she wanted and left her alone. He settled in a nearby chair and brooded. He wanted back the sweet, warm, giving woman that had lost herself in his arms.

CHAPTER 20

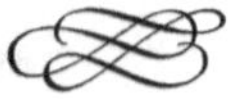

Agnieska couldn't look Stan in the eyes. Not after what had happened earlier this morning, when she'd acted like a wanton hussy.

When he'd fallen asleep, she'd taken the chance and worked herself out from his embrace. Confused about everything that had happened, she grabbed her discarded clothing and fled the bedroom and the house, her shame following her as she ran over to Malgorzata's house to ask for some guidance.

No one had ever told her how pleasurable the act could be, and she'd been completely unprepared for what had happened. There had to be something wrong with her.

Malgorzata had been married for more than twenty years, borne five children, Tadzio and Lola the nestlings still living at home. She would surely be able to shed some light on this delicate affair and how Agnieska should have reacted to all the indecent things Stan had done to her body. The mere memory made her flush with embarrassment and she brushed the thoughts away, hoping to gain some wisdom from the older woman.

But as she arrived at the house, the vile gossip Tekla Kozlow, a neighbor from further down the road, was visiting with Tadzio's mother. Agnieska hated the woman who'd been responsible for so much suffering, and wanted to slink away, but the other woman had already seen her.

"Come in, come in. Aren't you Agnieska Soban, the Jewess?"

Agnieska nodded silently.

"And wasn't your sister the girl who got impregnated out of wedlock by one of the Zdanek boys?"

Agnieska glared daggers at the vile woman, who didn't seem to notice, because she was too busy spreading her vitriol.

"The Zdanek boys can't be trusted. No decent woman would want to be seen with them. Am I not right, Malgorzata?"

Tadzio's mom tried to appease the other woman and said, "Tekla, I think you're being unjust. Peter and Ludmila were in love and they were young. Haven't we been reckless, too, back in the day?"

"Reckless? Me? I'm not a whore cozying up to every soldier passing through town like some of the young girls do..." Then Tekla turned her head and peered at Agnieska. "I'm worried about you, my dear. You're living alone under one roof with this man and your reputation is already being questioned in town. No honest woman would do this, and I can only advise you to leave his house sooner rather than later if you ever hope to catch a good husband for yourself."

Out of sheer politeness to Malgorzata, Agnieska didn't

strangle the other woman and forced a smile on her lips. "Stanislaw is a very kind man."

"Oh! I should have known. He already convinced you to tend to his baser needs. Shame on you!"

Agnieska felt herself flush red and hot, but she was unable to utter a single syllable. Because Tekla was right. A modest woman waited until she was married, before she let a man do more than hold her hand.

"Tekla! That is enough. Don't you dare insult Agnieska in my house! She would never act like that," Malgorzata said.

But I did act like that.

Malgorzata had meant well, but her words confirmed the burning shame that already enveloped her. No decent woman would ever do what she had done. Agnieska left soon after and ran from Malgorzata's house as if the devil personified was behind her.

Now, she was back in Stan's house, preparing dinner for them. She'd been afraid he'd chase her off the yard for her shameful behavior this morning, but instead he'd come up to hug her as if what had happened between them wasn't completely embarrassing – awful even.

She resisted the urge to turn around and look at his handsome face. Guilt ate at her as she finished fixing their dinner. She did her best to behave normally as they ate, but it was impossible to forget what had happened a few feet above their heads. She shrugged off all his attempts to make her talk about what was upsetting her, until he finally gave up and excused himself as soon as they finished eating.

"Good night. I'd better turn in early. There's a lot of

work to do tomorrow," he said as he left the house through the back door.

Agnieska longed to call him back, but that would only lead to her succumbing to his kindness. And she knew without a shadow of a doubt that the moment he wrapped her in his strong arms she'd be done for and would repeat the mistake from this morning. No, it was better to keep a distance. Actually, it would be best to leave the farm and find someplace else to live.

She retired to bed, not able to sleep. The sheets still smelled of Stan and every wrinkle in them made her acutely aware of what they'd done. If she stayed silent and listened, she could still hear her late mother's words scolding her older sister for the shame she'd brought upon the family by falling pregnant out of wedlock.

She swallowed with fear. Even though her mother wasn't there anymore, she'd never approve of Agnieska's scandalous behavior.

This is insane. I have to stop thinking about him.

But the night was long, and sleep proved elusive. When morning arrived, she had barely slept and one glimpse into the mirror showed dark circles beneath her eyes.

Stan arrived for breakfast and she maintained her silence throughout. He had just left the kitchen, headed for the fields, when the sound of men's voices came from outside. She peered out the window and felt her heart stall.

A group of Soviet soldiers stood in the yard talking to Stan. She went to the doorway and when they saw her, they motioned her forward as well. Agnieska didn't have good past experiences with men in uniform and tried to hide the trembling in her hands by burying them in the folds of her skirt.

Stan gave her a meaningful look and then explained, “These men are asking for our papers.”

Agnieska swallowed and asked, “Why? Is something wrong?”

The man in charge answered her, “We are going to all of the outlying farms and checking papers.”

Agnieska looked back at the house. “Mine are inside.”

“Go and get them.”

She nodded and returned to the house even as Stan reached into his pocket and produced his own. Agnieska retrieved her paperwork from where it was stored in a kitchen drawer. Outside the officer gave them but a short glimpse and nodded, before pushing them back into her hands. Then he stared at Stan and demanded to know, “Why haven’t you joined the Polish Worker’s Party yet?”

The Polish Worker’s Party was a mere puppet to Stalin, and Agnieska knew how much hatred Stan held for the communists and the Soviets in general. She tucked her paperwork into her pocket, nervously awaiting Stan’s answer to the question.

“I wasn’t aware that everyone was expected to join the PPR,” Stan said with anger and defiance in his voice.

“Do you have a problem with the life-changing achievements of the great Stalin and his communist party?” the officer demanded.

Stan’s face grew cold and he stood a little taller. “And if I do?”

The officer didn’t take kindly to his stance and stared

him down. "Maybe you and I should discuss your problems with the communists further?"

Stan shook his head. "I don't think so. Last time I checked this was still Poland and not the Soviet Union. Now get off my property!"

Agnieska stifled a gasp and froze in shock as she witnessed how Stan turned on his heel and the officer put a heavy hand on his shoulder, whilst the other two soldiers pointed their rifles at Stan.

"I don't think so. You are coming with us. Take him," the officer demanded.

"You can't do this!" Stan shouted angrily.

"I can do anything I want."

"What are you? A stupid Nazi?"

The officer's fist landed against Stan's jaw and Agnieska cringed from the pain she saw in his eyes. *Why can't he just keep his mouth shut?* The four men had all but forgotten about her presence and she silently stepped out of the way when two of the soldiers dragged Stan toward their vehicle.

She watched the vehicle disappear with Stan, feeling desperation take hold of her. There was nothing she could do. She returned to the kitchen, washing the dishes, cleaning the floor. Then she tended to the gardens until Tadzio came rushing across the fields shouting happily, "Hey, do you know where Stan is? I want to show him something."

It broke her heart to tell him, so she didn't. "He had to go to town on an urgent errand. Will you be able to work on your own for the day?"

Tadzio nodded. "Sure. I'm almost a grown-up."

"That you are." She ruffled his hair and handed him

some carrots and a lettuce head before saying, "Bring this to your mother."

Agnieska spent the rest of the day listening for Stan's steps in the doorway. Each noise caused her to jump in expectation of his return, but each time it was a false alarm. Her worry increased with every passing minute. By mid-afternoon, she was nothing more than a bundle of frayed nerves and tears.

One could never be sure what happened when confronted with the authorities. He wouldn't be the first one to be sent to a work camp in Siberia.

CHAPTER 21

The soldiers took Stan straight to the town hall in Lodz, where they interrogated him. The room looked eerily familiar. Blank walls. A single bare lightbulb hanging down from the ceiling. A lone chair sat in the middle of the room, handcuffs attached to either side of the tall back.

They shoved him down into the chair but didn't attach the cuffs. A man in a military uniform entered together with a civilian – some local party member eager to serve his Soviet masters. Stan cringed as he anticipated the agony ahead.

The Polish man began firing questions at him rapidly, while the Soviet officer stood there motionless.

"It has been brought to our attention that you haven't joined the Polish Worker's Party. Is that right?"

"Yes." Stan opted for saying as little as possible.

"Why?"

"Because I'm a farmer and was busy cultivating my fields."

The other man raised an eyebrow. "Are you sure you aren't a sympathizer of the traitorous Home Army?" Many of the farmers in Poland had been supporters of the Home Army that had quickly fallen into disgrace with Stalin, because they wanted an independent Poland.

"I'm certainly not." That was a lie. Stan had been fighting with the Home Army partisans throughout the war.

"Where are your loyalties?" The interrogator asked.

"With my country."

"And still, you resist joining the great PPR? How's that?"

Stan shook his head. "I'm a simple farmer."

"A farmer? Or a collaborator with the Nazis?"

"I would never collaborate with those damned bastards!" Stan shouted.

"Why don't you like the communists?" the Soviet officer intervened.

"I never said I disliked them." As Stan's anger mounted, his patience hung on a thin thread.

"Then you won't have a problem signing this party affiliation."

"I do have a problem with you forcing my hand," Stan hissed, running a hand through his cropped hair. How on earth had he ended up in this nightmare? Again? Last time he checked the occupation was finally over.

"Look, if you know what is good for you," the local part functionary lowered his voice to a threatening whisper, "you will sign this paper. Or…"

"Or what?" Stan couldn't contain his indignation anymore and jumped up. "Are you threatening me?"

"No. We're merely pointing out the consequences of your actions. Sign the paper and return to your farm right now or defy the authorities and find yourself on the next transport to a Gulag in Siberia. What will be your choice?"

Those damn bastards were serious. But Stan wouldn't be true to himself if he weren't as stubborn as he was short-tempered. For a short moment Agnieska's image appeared in front of his mind, but even her pleading face couldn't make him succumb to their extortion. He'd never in his life join the communist party, just like he'd never collaborated with the Nazis. He'd rather die in a Russian work camp than betray his inner convictions.

"I'd rather rot in a Gulag than support you bastards!" he shouted.

"Take him to the NKVD, maybe he'll change his mind after a few days of their hospitality," the Soviet officer said and two soldiers jumped forward to drag Stan out of the room. The mention of the NKVD caused a shudder to run down Stan's spine. They were the Soviet equivalent to the Gestapo and prisoners in their *care* rarely came out in one piece.

For now he focused on staying upright, because his stump had gone numb from sitting in the chair for so long. He stumbled helplessly as they hauled him forward, struggling to regain his footing.

"Hey! Where are you taking the cripple?" a voice called out.

Stan squinted his eyes and saw the president of the farmer's association sitting in the dim hallway. As much as he'd tried to keep appearances up, obviously people knew about his leg.

"What do you mean, cripple?" one of the soldiers asked, turning his head to look at Stan with disgust.

"Came home from the war with only one leg. Don't tell me you fellas didn't know. Are you sleeping on your job?"

The two soldiers looked at each other, unsure what to do. After a while one of them said, "Let's take him back and ask the colonel." They hauled him back into the interrogation room, where the Soviet colonel and the Polish functionary were discussing something.

"What now?" asked the officer gruffly.

"Sorry, sir. But this man here… he has only one leg."

"Stupid fools! And you believe him? How would he be able to walk with only one leg?" the Polish man asked.

"We'll take a look. Strip."

Stan stood there dumbfounded, hating the man who'd brought his condition to their attention. He hadn't wanted to tell the bastards about his deformity for fear they would use it against him.

"Strip or we will do it for you," the officer said, pulling out a billy club and slapping it against his thigh.

Slowly, filled with embarrassment and a healthy dose of fear, Stan removed his work pants, revealing his wooden leg and the stump it was attached to.

Rowdy laughter broke out in the room.

And if that wasn't shameful enough, they forced Stan to sit down and remove the prosthesis so that they could see the pathetic remainder of what at one time had been a healthy human leg. Through it all, Stan clenched his jaw and held onto his temper.

"He's only half a man," one of them burst out laughing. "What should the NKVD do with him? Cut off the other leg?" Stan wished for the earth to open up and swallow him whole, while the four men cracked joke after joke at his expense.

"The party doesn't want people like him," said the PPR official.

"Neither does the Soviet Union have use for him in one of the labor camps," added the Soviet officer and finally ordered, "Let him go."

Stan silently reattached his wooden leg, dressed and slinked away with his shoulders hunched and his eyes cast to the floor – doing anything but meet the eyes of people either ridiculing or pitying him.

The initial relief he felt at being turned loose quickly transmuted into red-hot fury. Ire like he hadn't felt in a long, long time took hold of him and he entered the first bar he came across with the goal of getting pissed until he blacked out.

From experience he knew hard liquor was the only way to stop the emotions ravaging his heart and soul. He couldn't bawl like a woman, and neither could he start a brawl like a real man, so he had to resort to the numbing effects of vodka.

CHAPTER 22

Agnieska was sick with worry. The night had long since settled over the land, casting the road leading up to the farm in an eerie moonlight. Why didn't they let Stan go? Given his reputation for fits of rage, she could only imagine how bad it had gotten. And there was absolutely nothing she could do to help him.

She paced the bottom floor of the house, jumping at every little noise, quickly moving past concern to full panic. Way after midnight, she accepted the futility of her pacing and went upstairs, where she finally fell into a troubled sleep. Early in the morning she woke with a start and rushed downstairs to look for Stan. Nothing. She rushed over to the shed and peered inside. Nothing.

Despair grabbed at her heart with an icy hand. *Where is he? What have they done to him?* When he didn't return by mid-morning, she took her coat and handbag and walked out of the door, determined to find him.

Once in town, she headed straight for the town hall. Usually she avoided going to town at all costs except on market day, because she feared running into some of the persons that had worked for the Nazis and mistreated her during her time in the Lodz Jewish Ghetto. *That's over now. The Nazis are gone,* she kept saying to herself as she squared her shoulders, bracing herself for an unpleasant encounter with the past.

Nothing happened, not until she reached the big courtyard in front of the registry office, where an unusual number of people milled about, apparently waiting for something to happen. She had to work her way through the crowd to reach the entrance door. Just as she arrived at the stairs, someone recognized her. It was a Polish policeman, who used to work for the Nazis, ratting out Jews in hiding.

"Another Jewish pig! You dare to return to this place?"

Fear seized Agnieska by the heart and she ducked her head. Had she really survived the Nazis and all of the horrors brought about by them during the war, just to be forced to endure it all over again?

"Haven't you got the message that we don't want you here?" someone else shouted.

"I'm a Pole, just like you," she said, trying to make her way up the stairs and inside the town building.

"You're a filthy Jew and you should have died along with the others!"

"Yes, the one thing Hitler got right was ridding us of your kind," a man spat at her and the blood froze in her veins, horrible memories rushing back at his vicious actions. She wrapped her shawl tighter around her shoulders and bolted up the stairs, reaching for the door into safety, when she felt a heavy hand on her shoulder.

"Not so fast, pig," a hateful voice said and thrashed her to the ground.

Wincing, she protected her head as kicks and punches hailed down on her. She was sure the mob would lynch her, and mumbled a prayer. As if to answer her prayer, a shot cut through the air and the mob scrambled for cover, leaving her bloodied and hurting on the ground.

Moments later two policemen approached her with another man in tow. One of the policemen helped her up, asking, "Can you walk?"

She bit down on her lips at the stabbing pain in her ribcage, but managed to get up and put on a brave face. "I guess so. Thanks for your help."

"Just glad we arrived in time, since those people are not to be trifled with." The second man gave her a compassionate look.

"Agnieska? What in the world are you doing here?" Stan said, stepping out from behind the two policemen.

"Looking for you," she answered between gritted teeth.

"You know this woman?" the first policeman asked, turning to look at a quite disheveled Stan.

"Yes. She's my sister-in-law. She's living up on the farm with me."

The two men gave Stan a look she couldn't decipher and the taller one said, "I'm Mikos and this is Andrej. We used to be with Stan in the same partisan unit."

"Thanks for saving me," Agnieska said.

"That's our job. But anti-Semitism is still rampant around here and you'd better be careful." Mikos cast a glance at Stan and added, "If you'd only join the Worker's Party, both of you would be so much safer. The communists are grappling for power and with Stalin having their back it'll only get worse for everyone else."

Stan shot his friend a dark stare, but Mikos only laughed. "You know I'm right, whether you like it or not."

"If you want a peaceful life, think about joining the PPR. It's just a piece of paper," Andrej said.

"Over my dead body," Stan hissed with barely concealed rage.

"Very nearly it was over her dead body." Mikos pointed at Agnieska, who could feel the bruises forming on her battered body.

"Sad as it is, your relative won't be safe in this town until she marries a good Catholic man, who'd better be a party member."

"She's a good-looking woman who seems to cook well," Andrej said after a look at Stan's healthy appearance. "We could arrange for her to meet some eligible suitors."

"No!" Stan all but shouted, and Agnieska had to bite back a smile.

They bid their farewells and then walked silently back to the farm. Every step sent a stabbing pain through her and she pressed her hand against her ribcage.

"You sure you can walk all the way home?" Stan asked, stopping for a moment and looking into her eyes, which were filled with pain. "Poor thing." He stood directly in front of her, his face mere inches away from hers. His glacial blue eyes softened as he reached out his hand to put a strand of hair behind her ears.

That was when she smelled it. Alcohol. She backed away and asked, "Where were you last night?"

"Out."

"Out? I was worried to death and you were out and drinking?" She itched to slap him across the face. Hard.

CHAPTER 23

Stan saw the hurt, pain and anger in Agnieska's eyes and felt like a piece of shit. Again, he'd been so caught up in his own suffering, consumed by self-pity, that he'd not even given a thought to the anguish she must feel when he'd stepped foot inside the bar the night before.

What kind of man drank himself unconscious while the woman he loved was at home fearing for the worst? Her seagreen eyes had turned into a dark ocean agitated by a violent storm, the anger rolling off of her in waves. If she'd known he was out drinking instead of being detained in a prison or worse, she wouldn't have come looking for him.

And she wouldn't have run into the mob trying to lynch her. The bruise forming on her cheekbone made him all too aware that it was solely his fault. Because of him she'd been attacked, beaten up and hurt.

"Agnieska, I'm sorry," he said after looking at her for a long time. "I'm so sorry."

She pinned him with her angry glare. "You are sorry? I

was worried to death that those bastards would send you to Siberia or worse! How dare you hurl your trite apologies! How about you grow up and think about anyone else besides yourself!"

Tears of fury coursed down her cheeks, but Stan knew better than to try and comfort her right now. She spun around, taking up the walk back to the farm. Agnieska refused to talk to him for the remainder of the day and even went to sleep without wishing him goodnight. He knew he needed to apologize in a big way. Just how?

The next morning he woke extra early and caught a ride into town, where he visited a few old friends and contracted with them to finish the roof. Then he made the trip to Malgorzata's house seeking advice.

"Hello?" he said, standing in the open doorway.

"I'm so glad they let you go," Tadzio said with a broad smile. Obviously, in a small place like this news travelled fast.

"Yes, they let me go."

"I hate the communists! Why don't we fight against them like we fought against the Nazis?"

Yes, why? Because people were tired after six years of oppression and war? Because many of the able-bodied men had been killed, maimed or were plain and simply too wrung out to take to the weapons and fight off another enemy?

"I'm not sure," Stan answered. "I was hoping I could speak to your mother for a few minutes."

"I'll get her for you. I was just getting ready to head over to your house. You have to see all the work I did yesterday!" Tadzio beamed with pride, pulling at Stan's heartstrings.

The poor boy hadn't seen his father and older brothers in years, and nobody knew their fate. For the first time it occurred to him that Tadzio saw a father figure in Stan, and that thought scared the hell out of him.

He was barely able to keep up appearances and hold his own life together; how could he serve as a role model to a thirteen-year-old fatherless boy?

Malgorzata wiped her hands on her apron as she entered the small hallway. "Stanislaw, come in. You gave us quite a fright!"

His ears burnt with shame. Two more persons had been worried about him, all because of his reckless behavior. "I'm sorry. I guess I should have kept my mouth shut when those thugs came to ask about my papers."

Malgorzata gave him a long once-over and then said, "Would you like some coffee?"

"Yes, please." He followed her into the kitchen, thinking about how to best broach the topic that weighed heavily on his heart. Nothing better than biting the bullet, he decided, and said, "I came looking for advice."

She poured him a cup of coffee and smiled. "About Agnieska?"

"H... how did you know?" he stammered.

"Let's just say life experience."

"She's still livid, because I drank myself into a stupor last night instead of coming home…"

"…and you feel guilty, for making her worry." She finished his sentence.

"That, and… she was brutally beaten up when she came looking for me…" He stopped.

"I heard of an incident, but didn't know the identity of

the poor woman," Malgorzata said, putting a hand to her chest. "Will this never end?"

"Friends of mine are with the police and we luckily came along to prevent..." He couldn't even consider what might have happened. "Anyhow, my friends said the only way to keep her safe around here was for her to marry a good Catholic man."

"So, what are you waiting for?"

"What? Me?"

"Don't you fancy her?"

He sighed. "I do. But... I'm not sure she'll ever forgive me for getting her into that situation."

"Stanislaw, that woman adores you and I can understand why she's livid right now. Seeing you hauled away by those men must have scared her to death. You have heard what happens to those who oppose the communists, haven't you? When you didn't return she assumed they'd already handed you over to the NKVD."

"I... I told her I'm sorry."

"A simple sorry won't cut it. You'll have to assure her that you are able to rein in your temper."

"It's just... I was so angry at the way they treated me." He stubbornly pushed out his lower lip, even though he knew his temper was at the root of the awful situation with Agnieska.

And everything else.

"Hear me out, young man," Malgorzata said with a stern voice, transporting him back to his adolescent years when he stood cowed in front of his mother as she scolded him for stirring up yet another brawl. "It's time for you to grow up and get a hold of that nasty temper of yours."

"But—"

"Don't interrupt me, young man. Did you know that half of Lodz used to be afraid of you because of your nasty temper? Especially the girls."

Stan shook his head. He'd known that most of the girls gave him a wide berth or avoided him all together, but he'd assumed it was because they'd rather spend time with his twin. Did… was… he realized it would kill him to find out that Agnieska feared him. He never meant to make her feel uncomfortable; he just had such a damn difficult time keeping his rage under control.

Malgorzata continued her lecture, but he couldn't hear her words, overcome with a desire to return to the house and beg Agnieska for forgiveness.

When he got there she wasn't in the garden and she wasn't in the kitchen.

"Agnieska?" he yelled into the eerily empty house, but no answer came. Then he heard steps coming down the stairs and she stood in front of him, fully dressed with coat, kerchief and a sling bag across her shoulder. "What are you doing?"

She looked into his eyes, her expression a mask of pain. "I can't stay here. Not after what happened yesterday." The graveness in her voice gave him the impression her decision to leave was about much more than his letting her down.

"Please… why do you leave?"

"It's not safe here for me."

Now he got the idea. "I will protect you from anyone trying to hurt you. I promise," he said hoarsely.

"You? Remember that I went to the town hall because I was worried about you?"

Shame flushed his face and made his ears burn. "I'm sorry. I really am. It will never happen again."

"You're right. It won't. Because I'm leaving." She stubbornly pushed out her lower lip but he'd perceived the slight tremble in her voice, nonetheless. Maybe he still had a chance to dissuade her.

"Agnieska... where will you go? If you have a safe place to go, I'll take you there."

She visibly choked at his words. "I... I just want to get away from those people," she finally whispered.

"Please. Don't endanger yourself. Stay with me for a while longer. Only until you've found a safe place to live." He could see her wavering and pressed on, "The farm is far enough away from town, so nobody will harm you here."

"It's not just about them, it's about us, too," she said, her voice thick with hurt.

"Swee... Agnieska, please. I'm so sorry. My behavior was awful. Inconsiderate. I never wasted a thought about how much you must have been worried about me." He stopped and scratched his beard, carefully forming the next sentences in his head. "I guess... I was on my own for so long that it didn't even occur to me someone could be worried about me."

"But I was... so much." Her rigid body melted just a tiny bit, encouraging him to approach her.

"We can make this work. Please stay. I promise," he said and her body melted some more. "I'll protect you." He reached out and put a hand on her shoulder, but she shrank back, knocking it off. Hurt – and fear – stabbed at his heart. Was Tadzio's mother right and the woman he loved feared him?

"Agnieska, are you afraid of me?" Stan asked, full of worry.

She looked at him in confusion. "Of course not. Why would you think that?"

"I went to see Malgorzata. She told me all of the girls were afraid of me..."

"...when you were much younger." Agnieska smiled, filling his heart with hope.

"Were you?" he asked, searching her eyes for the truth.

"Honestly, I was. A little bit. Perhaps a lot. Actually, I was terrified of you."

"Are you still afraid of me?" He swallowed hard.

"Do I look afraid?" she laughed, her eyes blinking with mischief. To be honest, she didn't, which was a great relief, but he had to hear it in her own words.

"Please tell me you're not afraid of me. I couldn't stand causing you such anguish." Stan wanted to put that stubborn strand of chestnut hair behind her ear, but didn't dare to touch her.

She squinted her eyes at him, but acquiesced. "I stopped being afraid of you many years ago. We've both grown up since."

"So why did you shrink back when I put my hand on your shoulder?" he asked.

CHAPTER 24

"Because..." Agnieska stared into his bright blue eyes, thinking that she could continue to do so all day long. She longed to have him sweep her into his arms and kiss her worries away, but there were too many things still hanging between them.

"Because?"

"I don't want a protector. I want my freedom. My independence. I want a life without being pushed around by others who have power over me. I have lived under the Nazi boot for so long, I'm sick and tired of others telling me what to do." Agnieska unloaded her entire soul onto Stan.

He smiled, only infuriating her more. What did this insupportable man think?

"Agnieska. Sweetheart. I need you as much as you need me," he said with a pleading tone in his voice, carefully approaching her again and taking her hand in his.

She looked down at her tiny hand covered by his big

one. A warm feeling flooded her body. And that indecent tingling again. But she wouldn't give in that easily. Not her.

"I don't—" she said through clenched teeth, but he put a finger on her lips to silence her. A rough, calloused finger that scratched her delicate skin, and for a moment she was tempted to succumb. But this was too important to be side-tracked by the sensations his touch always caused.

"Please hear me out," he said. "I know you're perfectly capable of living on your own. You are the strongest, most determined, most resilient woman I've ever met. And I wouldn't want you any other way. You're the first woman ever to stand up to me and put me in my place when my temper has overwhelmed me. Therefore, I need you. I want to be a better man. For you."

Tears sprang to her eyes and she couldn't respond.

"I love you," he said, putting a soft kiss on her lips. Delirious joy rushed through her veins and she thought she'd faint in his arms.

"You love me?" she whispered when he finally released her mouth to come up for air.

"Yes. I was too busy wallowing in self-pity to notice it right away, but I've loved you from the moment I saw you, lost and sad, on my porch."

She swallowed, unsure what he expected her to say. Or what she wanted to say. She was sure she loved him, too, but there was something inside her that held her back.

"I may not be everything you deserve, because I'm just a simple farmer who got his life education by fighting with the partisans. But I promise I will take care of you and cherish you every day of my life."

It didn't take more than that, and the most resilient woman he knew crumpled into his arms, begging him to kiss her again. And again. And again.

"I love you, too," she said much later, when they lay beside each other in her bed, recovering from the sweetest lovemaking ever.

Her glance fell on the sheet, where he hid his amputated leg beneath the thin cloth. She worried her lip, wondering how she could convince him to trust her enough to show her his stump. It just felt so awkward that he was hiding this part of him from her, when they were lying naked beside each other. But every time she'd teased her hand down that side, he'd pushed it away.

"What has you so worried, my sweet woman?" He breathed into her ear, his forefinger straightening the wrinkle on her forehead she knew she was making with her frown.

"Let me see your stump."

He stiffened as if she'd punched him in the stomach. "Agnieska, I'd rather not."

"Why not?"

Stan sighed. "Because… it's not a nice sight… and…"

"Are you afraid I'll run away screaming and never return?" She'd said it as a lighthearted joke but from the shocked expression on his face she knew instantly she'd hit the nail on the head. She wrapped her arm around his waist to keep him from bolting off the bed. "I won't. But it's a part of you and I want to see it."

With determined fingers she traced a downward path, but he put his hand over hers, apparently hoping to distract her. But Agnieska glanced down at their intertwined hand

and her gaze caught the shape of his prosthesis beneath the sheet.

Before he could stop her, she knelt on the mattress and reached for the straps that secured the wooden leg.

"Agnieska..."

"Let me see, please. It's part of you." When he didn't say a word, she added, "Don't you trust me?"

"Of course I trust you, it's just..."

"Please."

With another deep sigh, he said, "Alright. Have a look. But don't say I didn't warn you." He chuckled, but she could see right through him and tell he was horrified.

She carefully unbuckled the wooden leg and set it aside, before she removed the tight sock-like garment around his leg. He'd told her the truth when he said it wasn't a pretty sight. The skin was red, puckered and scarred and she had to bite back a gasp. She lightly ran a hand across the delicate skin and looked up when he drew a sharp breath. "Does it hurt?"

"No, but it's sensitive." Her brave and courageous man lay there hiding that he was trembling with fear. Fear that she might love him less because he owned an ugly stump instead of a healthy leg.

Agnieska gave him a reassuring smile and placed a kiss on the stump, before she crawled up and relaxed into his arms. "Thank you for trusting me." She clasped his face and said, "I love you, Stan."

"I love you more," he said, holding her tight.

She giggled and raised her head to look into his wonderful blue eyes that were so full of love and joy.

The sound of the hens in the yard going wild because

nobody had been out to feed them or collect the eggs yet finally roused them from the bed. They dressed, taking time to exchange kisses and little touches, but they eventually made it downstairs to attend to the daily chores.

CHAPTER 25

Late in the evening, after catching up with their daily chores, Stan washed up outside at the well. For the first time since Jarek's death he whistled and a broad grin spread across his face as he spied Agnieska's silhouette moving about the kitchen through the window.

Despite the loss of his leg he was happier than ever before in his life. All because he loved her. *And she loves me.*

But then a sobering thought entered his mind. What if she didn't love *him,* but was only using him as a substitute for Jarek, the twin she'd once preferred? Jealousy at the man who'd been his other self for a quarter of a century threatened to slice his heart into pieces.

Nausea overcame him as he imagined Agnieska, in the arms of his brother. Or at least her imagining that he wasn't indeed Stan, but Jarek. Jarek had been so much more popular with the girls, despite sharing identical looks with Stan. But Jarek possessed a pleasant character, a down-to-earth, calm and friendly demeanor, and had served as the only anchor keeping brooding, hot-tempered, volatile Stan grounded.

He tried to replay every single moment of his time with Agnieska. Had she ever given a sign that she was still pining for Jarek? The uncertainty drove him crazy and he rushed to the shed to don a clean shirt before entering the kitchen.

She stood with her back to him at the stove, cooking their dinner. He so wanted to believe her love for him was true.

"I need to talk to you."

She spun around, her eyes full of fear. "What happened?"

"It's nothing bad." *Maybe.* "It's just… tell me about you and Jarek?"

"Jarek? Why?"

"I need to know."

She sighed and moved the pot to the side of the stove before she walked over to the table and sank down on one of the chairs. "It's been such a long time. I was sixteen. He was my hero. Handsome, intelligent, tender. I fell hard for him. But you know that because you were there."

He scrutinized her face for hidden traces that she was still in love with his dead brother. "Do you… do you miss him?" he asked with a feeble voice.

"Miss him? Yes."

He held his breath.

"But not because I still love him. I miss him the way I miss my sister and my friends."

He blew out a sigh of relief. "So you're not in love with him anymore?"

Agnieska locked eyes with him and he had the eerie feeling she could look right into his soul and uncover his darkest fears. She smiled, putting her soft and tiny hand on his. "What exactly are you afraid of, Stan?"

"Me? I'm not afraid."

"Liar." She rubbed her thumb against the rough skin on the back of his hand.

"Alright, I am afraid. I can't live with the idea that you love me only because I look like him."

"Stan, darling." She got up and sat on his lap, taking his chin in her hand and forcing him to look into her eyes. "Don't be stupid. I love you because you are Stan. I admit that in the beginning I compared you to Jarek quite often. But that stopped after a few days. The Jarek I knew was a boy. But you… you are a man. A wonderful man." She paused for a moment and added, "Nobody knows what would have happened if Hitler hadn't invaded Poland and started this awful war. Jarek might still be alive. But then, neither you nor I would be the people we have since become. The war and our experiences have shaped us and while we weren't a good fit for each other back then, I think we go well together now."

Stan wanted to weep at her wonderful declaration of love, but since he was a man, he tamped down the vulnerable emotions. Instead he kissed her on her lips and murmured against her mouth, "I love you so much."

He took his time, savoring the intimate contact. His hands slid to her waist and from there slowly beneath the edge of her blouse.

"Agnieska. Love. You are so beautiful," he murmured, his hands on her flat stomach.

"Not here," she whispered with heated cheeks that made her all the more desirable.

"Nobody will see us."

"But it's not right. We shouldn't..." Reluctantly he removed his hands from under her blouse and she leaned her back against his chest. "We really shouldn't..."

"Shouldn't what?" he asked, nibbling at her earlobe.

Heat flushed her neck, ears and cheeks and she writhed on his lap. "Shouldn't enjoy this so much?"

He stopped in his tracks and broke out into laughter. "Why on earth shouldn't we enjoy making out? Isn't that the whole purpose of it?"

Her face took on the color of a beet; any brighter and she could serve as an alarm signal. "No... no... that... that is scandalous."

Stan didn't believe his ears. "What are you talking about?"

"It's just that a decent woman wouldn't... you know... do all those things we did... and she definitely never would... put her mouth on..."

"My dick?" he said, amused by the expression of utter shock in her face.

"Stan, please!" she hissed.

"I liked it. A lot."

After a long silence she said, "That's exactly what I'm talking about. I was raised in a very traditional way and until you, all I knew about these things was that it was a wife's duty to please her husband in bed."

"Things have changed, sweetheart." He caressed her shoulder, hoping to calm her pricks of conscience.

"But it isn't right."

"I understand you were raised to think being with a man is merely a chore and not something a woman would enjoy, but I assure you, there's nothing wrong in what we did. Don't you believe that I enjoy making love to you so much more when you enjoy it too than if you'd be lying there like a rag doll overcome with guilt and shame?"

She looked at him slightly doubtful. "Is this true? Does it make a difference for you?"

He bit back a chuckle. "It makes a hell of a difference. I'd say it's like comparing bland potatoes to one of your delicious potato stews."

"Hmm…" she murmured and he could see the wheels spinning in her head, trying to process their conversation.

"What else do you want to know?" he asked, wrapping his arms around her.

"Have you done this before? Slept with a woman?" she finally asked with a soft voice, barely above a whisper.

Stan nodded. "Living with the partisans in the woods, it was all we talked and dreamed about. There were always enough willing women offering themselves, but it was never love. It was always business. I had no idea that it was a million times better if the heart's involved."

"So you don't think I'm a harlot?" she whispered.

"You? A harlot? Agnieska, you're anything but. The women offering themselves to any and all of the partisans, they were harlots. But not you."

She leaned back, snuggling against his chest, but he could tell she was still upset.

"Should we have dinner?" he finally asked and she nodded, getting up from his lap and putting the pot back on the stove again.

As he watched her aptly working in the kitchen, he started to worry about her. Her status as a Jew and a single woman offered her little to no protection. Both his friends and Malgorzata had offered the solution.

Marriage.

He'd never seen himself as a married man, and he'd certainly not considered himself deserving of a wonderful woman like Agnieska. He had nothing to offer her, except for his devotion and his name. Stan could turn around the issue as he liked, but there was only one way.

"Marry me," he blurted out.

"What?" She dropped the dirty plates into the sink and spun around, her eyes wide with surprise.

He walked over to her, took her hands in his own and said, "I can't kneel down, I don't have a ring and my farm might soon belong to the state. All I can offer you are my name and my protection."

Doubt flashed in her eyes. "You're not doing this because your friends said I needed the protection of a Christian husband?"

"No. Maybe. Alright, I normally wouldn't have proposed so soon." This was more difficult than he'd expected. Shouldn't any woman be grateful when a man offered her his hand in marriage? Then he remembered that she didn't want to be protected, subdued. She wanted to stand on her own two feet and he'd given her all the wrong reasons for his proposal.

"I'm sorry. I was trying to explain to you the rational side, when my feelings for you are anything but rational. I love you and I need you. Before you showed up on my porch I was lost. Depressed. Unhappy. Many times I asked myself whether it was even worth living another day."

She opened her mouth and he laid a gentle finger over her lips. "Let me finish, please?

"But everything changed with you. You gave me a reason to live. To be happy again. To work on controlling my temper. To be the best man I can be. For you. My first thought in the morning is about you, as is my last thought before falling asleep at night, and all my thoughts in between." He smiled. "Agnieska Soban, will you make me the happiest man on earth by agreeing to marry me?"

Agnieska looked at him and then she touched his cheek. "You really love me?"

"With all of my heart. Please say yes."

"Yes, yes, I will marry you. I was so lost before coming here. I didn't think I'd ever feel safe again. I felt so alone..."

"You'll never be alone as long as I'm here," he said in a trembling voice, unable to hide his emotions, and then he wrapped her in his arms. He dipped his head and took her lips with his own.

CHAPTER 26

Agnieska's head swirled with emotions, and Stan's kiss added butterflies in her stomach to the mix.

"Stan?" she murmured.

"You want to go upstairs and celebrate our betrothal?" His insistent hand had worked its way beneath her blouse.

"I want… but… don't you think we should get married first?"

His hand stopped cold. "You want us to go into town and get married right now? We can pick this back up when we return," he asked with a loving smile on his face. The prospect of getting into town was scaring the hell out of her and she shook her head in fear.

"So, I'll go and sleep in the shed," he said, disappointment evident in his voice.

"Wait, you don't have to…" Agnieska didn't want him to leave. Wanted to stay wrapped up in his arms. Sleep by his side all night and wake up in his arms. "Can't you come up and we just kiss?"

He chuckled. "As if that would work. No, sweetheart, my memory of what happens when we are kissing on your bed is still too fresh to believe that for one moment either one of us could hold back."

She sighed. Unfortunately, he was right. To hell with traditions! There was nothing wrong with making love to the man she'd soon be married to.

"I don't want you to go," she said, emboldened by her decision. "And I don't want you to hold back. I love doing these… things… with you. Because I love you."

He smiled. "Are you sure?"

"As sure as I can be after twenty-five years of believing otherwise. But I may still struggle a little not to feel guilty about feeling like this with you."

"You're a fast study, my love," he chuckled. "I would swoop you up in my arms and carry you upstairs if I could."

She smiled. "Walking up the stairs is something I can do perfectly well by myself, but making me feel safe and loved in your arms is something I can't do alone."

"Alright, woman. You walk upstairs and I'll take care of the protecting and loving for the rest of my life," he said, giving her a playful slap on her butt. "Go. I'll be right with you."

The next morning Agnieska woke early, because something heavy weighed her down. She moved and found Stan's arm tightly wrapped around her waist. With a smile on her lips she kissed him awake.

"Get up, lazybones, we have work to do."

He lazily opened his eyes and licked his lips when his gaze fell on her face. "Is it work we can do in bed?"

She giggled. "No. It's work you have to do dressed and out in the fields or we won't have food to eat come winter."

"It would be a shame for those gorgeous curves if we can't feed you properly," he laughed, and rolled out of bed.

Agnieska wondered whether this would be how she'd wake up every morning for the rest of her life. They ate breakfast and took care of the chores until noon, when Stan returned to the house with Tadzio, Malgorzata and little Lola in tow.

"What's up with that many guests?" Agnieska eyed him suspiciously.

"I promised to make an honest woman out of you," he chuckled. "And they're our wedding party."

For a moment Agnieska swayed at the notion of returning to the town hall, but Stan held her by the shoulders and whispered into her ear, "Don't be afraid, because from now on I'll protect you with my own life."

She was moved to tears.

"Ready to go? Our transport is waiting," he said and offered her his arm. They would go to the registry office for an unceremonious administrative act of signing a piece of paper and then return to the house to celebrate with their friends.

"Yes. Let's go get married." Agnieska wondered what kind of transport he'd arranged and as they stepped outside, she found a lorry full of hens waiting for them. She giggled and climbed into the driver's cabin, the man apparently a friend of Stan's from his time with the partisans.

"Congratulations. Would have bet all my worldly possessions that no woman would shackle our Stan. His brother, yes, but him? Anyhow, I'm happy for both of you."

Ten minutes later they arrived at the town hall and the driver promised to pick them up again in one hour. The clerk at the registry office didn't seem overly interested in them; he simply checked their passports and then signed their wedding certificate. "You are married now."

After the short ceremony, they walked out into the sunshine as husband and wife.

"What now?" Agnieska asked him.

"Since we have forty-five minutes left until Dariusz picks us up again, I'd like to go to the post office and send a telegram to Peter."

Agnieska stared at the crazy man who was now her husband.

"What's wrong with sending a telegram?" Stan asked, misinterpreting her shock.

"Nothing. But wouldn't Peter enjoy a letter explaining everything instead of a simple telegram saying 'Got married to Agnieska stop.'?"

Stan chuckled. "That's a woman thinking. What else would he need to know?"

Agnieska shook her head but decided to write a veritable letter during the next days with some details about their situation, the farm, the neighbors, and Poland in general.

When they returned home, a huge surprise awaited Agnieska. Thanks to the help Stan had procured days ago, the roof repairs had been completed and while they were gone, some helping hands had moved a huge marital bed into the master bedroom.

Agnieska wept with joy as she touched the fine wood and the soft linen sheets, no doubt a wedding gift from Malgorzata.

“She is a good woman,” Stan commented.

“She is. A good friend as well.”

“Let’s go celebrate,” Stan suggested and they climbed downstairs to meet Tadzio’s family in the kitchen with expectant faces.

Much, much later they retreated to their new bedroom with the much bigger bed. Agnieska looked at the man she loved so much and finally found the reason she had survived when so many had perished: to heal the broken spirit of this wonderful man with her love.

“I love you, Agnieska.”

She tipped her head up and kissed his jaw. “I love you right back. Thank you for keeping me here when I wanted to leave.”

“I will always be there for you, no matter what. Remember that.”

“Always.”

She was quiet for a few minutes and then her fingers started drawing circles on his chest. “Stan?”

“Yes?”

“This is a really nice, comfortable bed.”

Stan grinned and nodded. “Yes. Your point?”

“Well, I was thinking. We should probably consummate our marriage. Just in case. I mean, you promised to make an honest woman of me and you’ve yet to do that.”

“Oh, really? I thought marrying you made you an honest woman.”

“Well, in a manner of speaking. I think I’d like to see if married lovemaking is different than unmarried lovemaking.”

Stan rolled her beneath him and kissed her lingeringly. "There's only one difference that I know of."

"What's that?" she asked.

"I can actively try to impregnate you now. How many children would you like?"

"Children?" she asked on a squeak.

"I'd like a little girl who looks just like her mother."

Agnieska nodded and then smiled. "I think I'd like that too."

"It could take a while. We'll have to work extra hard and be persistent," he said with a smirk.

"I'm up for the challenge."

Stan met her eyes and she saw the love shining from them. "I will always be up for whatever challenges come our way."

*** The End***

Wait, don't go yet!

If you want to find out how Stan came to lose his leg and how he was saved from sure death, read Uncommon Sacrifice.

Uncommon Sacrifice is a book in my bestselling War Girl series, with plenty of action, history and some romance.

If you read only romance, then my other books written under my full name Marion Kummerow are not for you. But if you enjoy historical fiction with accurately researched history, action, suspense, and gripping love stories against all odds, I urge you to give my other series a try.

Thank you so much for reading Second Chance at First Love!

Marion Kummerow

ALSO BY MARION KUMMEROW

Love and Resistance in WW2 Germany

Unrelenting

Unyielding

Unwavering

War Girl Series

Downed over Germany (Prequel)

Blonde Angel: War Girl Ursula (Book 1)

War Girl Lotte (Book 2)

War Girl Anna (Book 3)

Reluctant Informer (Book 4)

Trouble Brewing (Book 5)

Fatal Encounter (Book 6)

Uncommon Sacrifice (Book 7)

Bitter Tears (Book 8)

Secrets Revealed (Book 9)

Together at Last (Book 10)

Endless Ordeal (Book 11)

Not Without My Sister (Spin-off)

Second Chance at First Love (romantic spin-off)

Berlin Fractured

From the Ashes (Book 1)

On the Brink (Book 2)

In the Skies (Book 3)

Into the Unknown (Book 4)

Against the Odds (Book 5)

Margarete's Story

Turning Point (Prequel)

A Light in the Window

From the Dark We Rise

The Girl in the Shadows

Daughter of the Dawn

Standalone

The Orphan's Mother

German Wives

The Berlin Wife

The Berlin Wife's Choice

The Berlin Wife's Resistance

Find all my books here:

http://www.kummerow.info

CONTACT ME

I truly appreciate you taking the time to read (and enjoy) my books. And I'd be thrilled to hear from you!
If you'd like to get in touch with me you can do so via

Facebook:
http://www.facebook.com/AutorinKummerow

Website
http://www.kummerow.info

www.ingramcontent.com/pod-product-compliance
Lightning Source LLC
LaVergne TN
LVHW091424190726
843491LV00006B/1600